A Time for SCANDAL

PREQUEL *to the* LADIES *of* WORTH

PHILIPPA JANE KEYWORTH

ISBN (eBook): 978-1-0684830-0-4

ISBN (Print): 978-1-0684830-1-1

ALSO BY
PHILIPPA JANE KEYWORTH

LADIES OF WORTH SERIES

A Time for Scandal

Fool Me Twice

A Dangerous Deal

Lord of Worth

Duke of Disguise

REGENCY ROMANCES

The Widow's Redeemer

The Unexpected Earl

MULTI-AUTHOR SERIES

Finding Miss Giles

FANTASY

The Edict

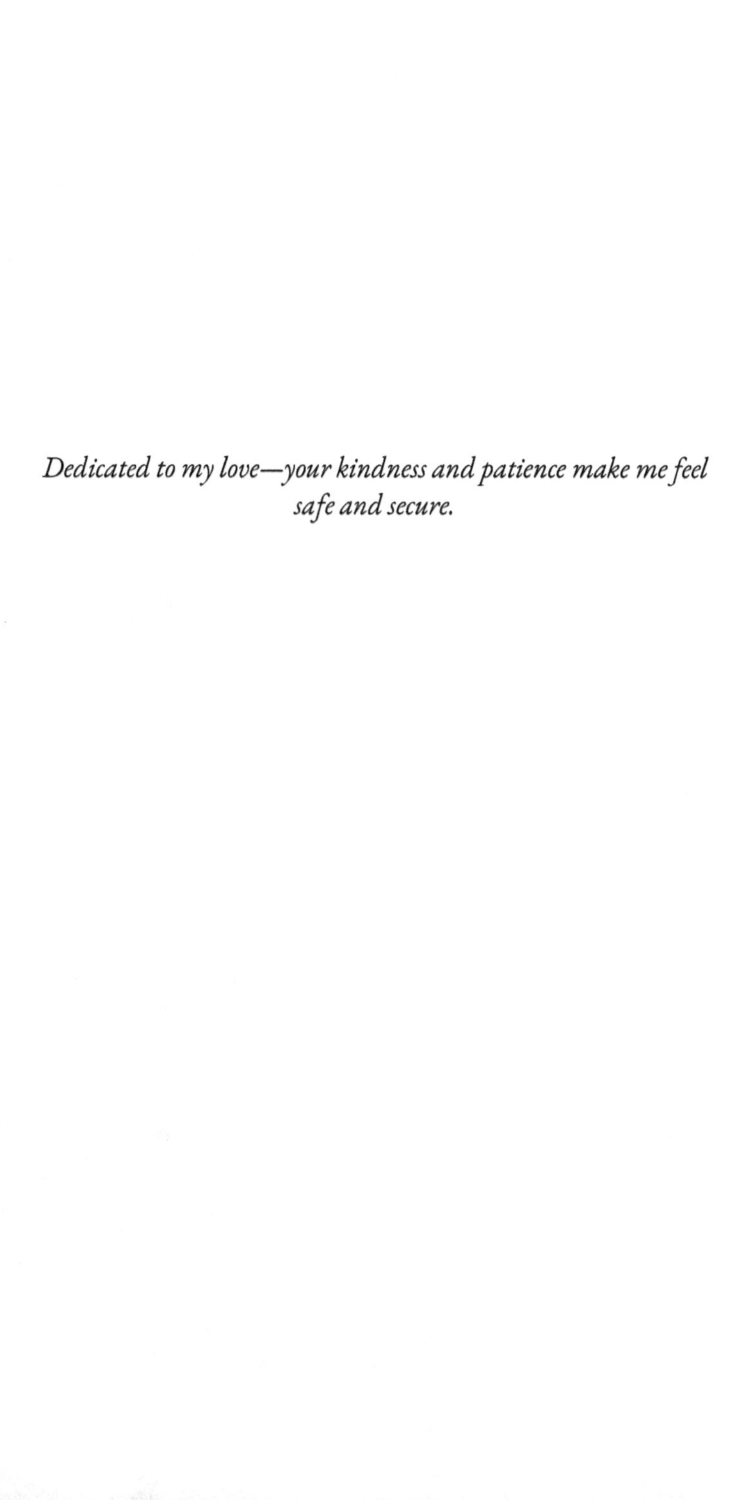

Dedicated to my love—your kindness and patience make me feel safe and secure.

CHAPTER 1

London, England 1739

Lord Standon was certain the young woman was talking to herself.

He had arrived late to the newly married Arleighs' ball and —after being accosted by half a dozen mamas and their husband-hunting daughters—he'd retreated here for respite.

The unused morning room had seemed the safe choice. Until he'd heard a voice. A feminine voice.

"I shan't let him come near you," it whispered.

Roderick scanned the candlelit room, his gaze catching on the figure of a young woman, attired in a finely embroidered blue and silver mantua. Her back towards him, he observed her fine waist, the intricately plaited and coiffured hair, and the fact she was talking to a portrait.

He considered his options. Return to the sea of noise and matrimonial expectations out in the ballroom—magnified as it was by the recent nuptials—or remain here with this... eccentric. Judging from her voice and figure, the woman was young, and despite appearing a little mad, Roderick deemed her the lesser of two evils.

She muttered something further to the ancestor of the current Viscount Arleigh, who was peering superciliously down at the room from his oil-painted world.

Roderick thought of taking up residence in one of the wing-backed chairs by the fireplace without greeting the room's occupant in the hopes of remaining unseen. However, he thought better of it.

If he did not alert her to his presence, there was no telling the fright he might inadvertently give her, and he had no desire to handle a screaming fit.

"Tell me, does the Viscount's portrait answer when you speak to him?"

The woman jumped, swinging round and locking sparkling blue eyes on him. To his surprise, she did not look frightened.

"How dare you!"

Yes, she looked most decidedly angry.

"I apologise for intruding on your tête-à-tête." Roderick bowed, thrown a little off kilter by those enigmatic eyes.

"My what?" she replied impolitely. Then, glancing behind her at the painting and after towards Roderick, she straightened and backed up.

Did the portrait just move?

The lady's furtive looks further piqued Roderick's curiosity. What *was* she up to?

"I hardly th-think it kind of you to make fun of me in such a fashion. Talking to oneself is most—clarifying for the mind. Don't *you* do it?"

The question was asked in such a way that if he was to reply in the negative, he would be declaring himself a fool.

His brows rose a fraction. Such forthright speech from a

young lady, and in such a compromising position in a room alone with a stranger. He was… intrigued. Roderick couldn't remember the last time he'd been intrigued.

"I confess"—he inclined his head in mock submission—"I have not indulged myself in that way before."

"Oh, but you must!" Her eyes were so bright and engaging, and she looked as though she wanted him to try talking to himself right there and then. "It is beneficial to consider one's thoughts in their entirety."

What was this lady up to?

She stepped back once more, her back against the wall.

Click!

The moment the click sounded, she strode forward away from the wall and its portrait, gesticulating wildly, and drawing his attention. "I would advise you to try it!" she said loudly.

Rather than coming near him, however, she kept a chair, then a table, between herself and Roderick as she traversed the room.

"Perhaps I should leave you to practise it?" she asked, glancing at the door.

Amusement hovered around Roderick's lips. He glanced at the wall and its portrait, observing the fine seam to the left of the gilt frame, confirming his suspicions. A secret door. A passageway, he had no doubt, that someone had just exited through. But who?

"I find myself at a disadvantage, Miss—?"

The woman in blue had manoeuvred him into the middle of the room with her skirting of the furniture. For every step he made towards her, she made one away. Soon she'd be out the door. The sly minx was outsmarting him!

"Then we are equally disadvantaged and does that not mean that neither of us are therefore disadvantaged at all?"

The absurd logic caught Roderick off guard, and he broke into unexpected laughter.

"There, you see the silliness of your statement yourself."

Still, she refused to give her name, and that made Roderick wish to know it all the more. Five minutes ago, he had wanted nothing but a silent retreat from the hubbub of the ball. Now he found himself completely entranced by this bizarre woman.

"You will not do me the pleasure of allowing me to know the name of this erudite philosopher before me?"

"I will not," she replied.

His attempts to waylay her were failing. He stepped forward and was about to say something further, but it was in vain.

"I shall leave you to practise clarifying your mind," she said, bestowing a smile upon him that did not meet her eyes. "Good evening."

Before he could say a word more, she opened the door and slipped out.

What an odd creature.

Roderick stared at the half-closed door for a full minute in contemplation. Then, coming to himself, he crossed the room to where the lady had been standing talking to the painting. He looked up into the stern countenance of an Arleigh ancestor. A moustache and neat little triangle beard decorated their face, and they wore a deep-fronted black silk suit with red-heeled shoes. Roderick's eyes dropped to the gilt frame, over and around it, and then to the nearby wall, where he had spied the hairline crack.

It was cleverly concealed amongst the stripes of the wallpaper. He reached up and ran a finger down its edge until, at about waist height, he felt the loop of a handle sitting flush with the paper. Its metal was painted to match the papers, so that one had difficulty spying it.

He eased it from its home with a thumbnail and pulled.

Click! The hidden door materialised from the surrounding wall, painting and all, and swung open before him.

Behind the concealed entrance was what could barely be described as a passage, for within less than two feet was another door. No doubt it led to the adjacent room in the Arleigh residence. Whoever the woman in blue had been talking to had already left by this second exit.

Closing the secret door again, Roderick rubbed his chin and frowned. He had thought this Season would be like the last, and the one before that, and the one before that. A time to be endured and matrimonial snares to be avoided. But this brief interlude had proven to be of a very different flavour.

Who was the lady in blue? And just who had she been talking to behind the secret door?

CHAPTER 2

"Have I told you Pen—he's just so handsome?"

Thalia *had* told Penelope. In fact, her sister had not stopped talking about Lord Fairing since breakfast. It was all because the gentleman in question had asked Thalia to dance twice at the Arleighs' ball last night.

"You've mentioned it," Penelope replied dryly, avoiding the temptation to say something cutting. "I have seen him myself, you know."

"He told me all about his horse called Major." Thalia ignored the sarcasm. "An enormous bay who can clear a six-foot hedge."

"He'd have to be a big beast to seat Lord Fairing."

They were progressing down Rotten Row in the morning sun at a leisurely pace, and so far, Penelope was not impressed by what she'd heard of her sister's new beau.

While Thalia had been supposedly romanced by the eligible Viscount Fairing, the great ox of a man had not asked a single question about her. Yet Penelope's younger sibling could recite everything about the gentleman, from a vivid description of the last hunt he'd been on, to what he'd studied at Oxford.

It was most galling that Thalia did not see the imbalance. How could she admire a gentleman who showed no interest in her?

No, that was not strictly true.

Lord Fairing had told Thalia she looked pretty. Penelope resisted the urge to roll her eyes at the thought.

"He is very tall," Thalia agreed, "and athletic." There was glee in her sister's voice. "When he danced with me, he held my hand so firmly and..."

This was the third retelling of the dances. Therefore, Penelope felt justified in allowing her mind to wander.

It went to where it had been running back to in every free moment since last night.

Lady Spencer.

It was a stroke of good fortune to be in the Arleighs' house when she had been approached by Lady Spencer, wanting to avoid a persistent suitor.

Anywhere else and Penelope wouldn't have known about secret doors to escape through. A childhood of playing with the Arleigh daughters, running amok through this house and slipping away through the cleverly hidden doors they'd shown her, had equipped her to help the beautiful stranger.

When the widow had begged Penelope's help, she had agreed at once. Her Ladyship had seemed genuinely shaken by this Count-something-or-other when she'd pointed him out. It didn't matter that Penelope hadn't been formally introduced to her Ladyship.

A woman in need could *not* be ignored.

And when Lady Spencer had squealed on shutting the door to the Arleigh morning room because she had seen the Count following them, Penelope had immediately thought of the hidden passageway.

What an odious man the Count appeared to be. He had been leering at her in a most abominable way.

"Ouch! Stop pinching my arm!" Thalia yelped, smacking Penelope's gloved fingers.

"Oh, sorry," said Penelope, releasing her grip on her sister's arm, and adding peevishly, "It's not like I meant to."

"What on earth was going through your mind?" Thalia had snatched her arm away and was holding it protectively, glaring at her elder sibling.

"Nothing really. I was just thinking about last night."

"Last night?" Thalia asked in shocked accents. "How could such a lovely ball make you look as though you had sucked a lemon *and* pinch your poor sister's arm?"

The question was rhetorical, and Penelope knew any attempt at answering it, even soothingly, would be foolish. Her sister needed to cool off. Nothing would do but to maintain silence in the hopes her temper would cool sooner and they could continue their walk.

Penelope's mind turned back to Lady Spencer. It was just so horrid remembering what the widow had said about Count... Feccio. That was his name!

Apparently, the Italian noble had shown an interest in Lady Spencer shortly after her husband had died last year in Italy. Improperly soon, in fact, and the widow was not interested. Originally from a wealthy family in Northumberland, and with no living relatives left in Italy, she had been driven from the Continent by the persistence of Feccio's suit and returned to London.

But Feccio had followed.

"Come on then," Thalia huffed, "or we shall lose Mother." She reluctantly offered her recently injured arm once again to her sister.

Penelope took it, and they continued along Rotten Row.

She spied their mother up ahead, who had gained some twenty yards on them now, chatting with a family acquaintance.

Had Lady Spencer managed to evade the Count for the rest of the evening? Penelope hoped so. If she hadn't been interrupted by… the interrupting gentleman—that is what she would call him—then she might have been sure as to the widow's success.

At least it hadn't been the Count. Penelope had almost jumped out of her skin when the interrupting gentleman had addressed her. But he'd been English. A quick question to her mother later in the evening had revealed he was Roderick Westbury, Lord Standon, heir to the Etheridge earldom, established bachelor and expert at avoiding matrimonial snares thrown out by scheming mamas.

Being Penelope's second Season, she had heard of him, but thus far, their paths had never crossed. No doubt down to his expert avoidance of eligible females. If they did in the future, she was sure he would now avoid her. After last night, he would most definitely consider her a suitable inmate for bedlam. It had suited her purposes at the time, and to be honest, even without talking to portraits, Penelope was well aware her family name was deterrent enough for eligible gentlemen. One wasn't the daughter of a suspected Jacobite sympathiser without consequences.

"Girls." Lady Harwood turned from her acquaintance to address her approaching daughters. "We should like to sit by the water for a moment."

Penelope and Thalia followed their mother's diversion obediently, departing from the main promenade down a path on which sat a bench beside the Serpentine.

Her sister was still going on about the ball. "I don't think I've ever had such divine turtle soup and—"

"Lady Spencer!" Penelope's voice cried out in a most unladylike manner. The widow was approaching from the opposite direction, accompanied by her maid.

"Gracious, Pen! You'll make my ears bleed!" cried Thalia, snatching her arm away from her sister for the second time and placing both gloved hands over her ears. "You are beastly."

"Oh, do hush, Thalia," Penelope hissed, striding forward to greet her new acquaintance. "How fortuitous to meet you, Lady Spencer."

The tall, slim widow was clad in a deep blue silk dress, the colour broken by fine white flowers—maybe roses—embroidered across her skirts. Her bodice was edged with blue and white taffeta in neat pleats, and on her perfectly curled and powdered hair, sat a bergère hat with matching silk flowers and ribbon.

"My saviour!" replied the widow, her large green eyes glittering enigmatically at Penelope and her rouged lips curving into an attractive smile. She held out her white-gloved hands to take both of Penelope's and squeezed them like they were old friends.

"May I present my sister, Lady Thalia." Penelope stepped back to allow Lady Spencer to greet her sibling.

"A pleasure, Lady Thalia, and a beauty just like your sister." Lady Spencer bestowed her winning smile on each lady in turn. "Perhaps you might allow me to steal your sister away from you for a few moments for a walk beside the river?"

Penelope felt a swell of pleasure at being asked for a private tête-à-tête by so elegant a lady. She was used to the tittle-tattle of her peers, always fawning over gentlemen just like her sister was a moment ago, with nothing of import to say. They were all so young. Not at all like the well-travelled Lady Spencer.

"I would be delighted," said Penelope, without consulting her sister. "Go and keep Mama and Mrs Thurzon company, Thalia."

Immune to the look of indignation on her sister's face at

being so summarily dismissed, Penelope took up Lady Spencer's offered arm and turned back the way her Ladyship had come.

"Harwood, you say? Must be the daughter of Earl Harwood. Terrible scandal."

Roderick had been breakfasting with his father when he'd asked if the Earl of Etheridge knew anything of the Harwood family. It had not taken much digging after the ball to find out the name of the young woman he'd interrupted while talking to a painting the previous evening.

"Cursed fool of a man—was friends with the Old Pretender."

The exiled Stuart heir to the throne? So it was *that* Harwood family. Roderick's intrigue deepened.

His father, who had been partaking of an exceedingly large plate of eggs and ham, always enjoyed the opportunity to hold court at the breakfast table. This topic set him in full sail.

"Converted to Catholicism—dashed popish nonsense," Lord Etheridge spat out with derision. "Got himself het up about the country being better off with a Catholic king and started up a kinship with the Stuart heir. Insisted on keeping up with him even after the mess of Sheriffmuir and loss at Preston. Said to have visited the Old Pretender as he lay sick with fever in Peterhead before leaving England. Rumour has it Harwood was entrusted with some of the Stuart jewels for safekeeping until the false king returns. A load of hogwash, of course!"

Roderick wasn't sure if his father meant the fabled treasure or the Stuart's claim.

The Earl's next words removed any doubt. "We shall never suffer a Catholic king again, thanks to the Glorious Revolution. The French could learn a thing or two from us, if they weren't so arrogant."

"And what of Harwood?"

"Died, a few years ago, if memory serves. Left behind him his wife and two daughters—of whom I assume you speak. Still in Society, are they? Great taint upon their names. Great taint. To be avoided, if you ask me."

Roderick hadn't.

The Harwood women holding little interest, his father turned back to his previous theme and blustered about the Stuart pretenders for the next quarter of an hour. That gave way to a soliloquy on the present King George and how the Earl of Etheridge was much liked at court.

Roderick tuned out this self-aggrandising after a few minutes, and Lord Etheridge required no rejoinder to his monologue. So, the young woman with the bright blue eyes talking to the painting was one of *those* Harwood women. He had not been formally introduced, but he'd heard plenty of tittle-tattle about the Harwood family before. The whole of Society had, though the gossip had certainly lessened in recent years. Hadn't his mother been friends with Lady Harwood before her husband's conversion?

After playing the attentive son, Roderick struck out for Rotten Row. He was on his way to meet his friend Mr Allen for chops and ale in a nearby tavern, when lo and behold, the blue-eyed Lady Penelope came across his path.

In truth, he detoured from the main thoroughfare when he spotted her to ensure said crossing of paths. After the conversation with his father that morning he was curious to know her better, and when he saw the widowed Lady Spencer in her company, he felt an interruption might be in order.

CHAPTER 3

"I must thank you," the widow said as soon as they were out of earshot of the others. "You were very kind to me last night—I confess, I had hoped to see you here to say so— you were strong when I was all weakness."

"Oh, nonsense!" said Penelope, a surge of pride making her chest swell. "I merely knew of a way for you to escape... well... you know—" She broke off, not wanting to say the gentleman's name. "How are you feeling this morning?"

"Better," Lady Spencer replied, a slight hitch in her voice. "I only worry that—oh, you were so kind to help me. Especially as you knew nothing of my character, and I just accosted you."

"I could see very well he was not a pleasant man," said Penelope earnestly. They passed some children and their nurse feeding ducks on the river. "It did not matter that I didn't know you."

"You are so good," Lady Spencer replied. "I find the man... oversets me."

"And—" Penelope paused, not wanting to risk this new-found friendship, but determined to help. "Can you not simply refuse the man?"

"I have tried, oh, how I have tried! But—" Faint colour appeared in Lady Spencer's cheeks. "But he knows... "

"I shall not say a word of anything you tell me," Penelope assured her, wishing to be a confidant, and feeling the gravity of the intimacies Lady Spencer was sharing.

She was unlike any of the friends Penelope had. She was a real woman, grown, married and widowed, having lived on the Continent and now back in England, presumably independent. How Penelope envied and admired her.

"You are too kind to me. I should not allow my new friend to worry over my problems. They are my own and I'm only thankful to have confided in a lady such as yourself in my hour of need. I knew a woman in Rome like you. She too was pretty, with blue eyes and quite the cleverest lady of my acquaintance."

Penelope wasn't sure what to say to the compliment. "It must have been wonderful to live in Rome."

How lame she sounded. But she meant it. She imagined the classical vistas and beautiful statues she had seen in etchings and books about the Eternal City. "I would love to go."

"One day you must. Wasn't your father fond of travel?"

Penelope's step faltered.

"Yes," she said quietly, regaining her pace. It had been several years since her father's death, but it still twinged when people mentioned him unexpectedly. "He travelled to Italy a few times."

It was her father who had brought back the books and etchings of Rome which Penelope had pored over as he described the architecture and places to her.

"I am sorry." Lady Spencer's tone softened. "I feel the same when speaking of my dear husband. It is why Count

Feccio causes me so much upset. He was friends with my husband, you see, and now he... he... *threatens* me."

"Threatens?!" Penelope snapped out of her maudlin reverie. "Whatever do you mea—"

"I've said too much," Lady Spencer said. "As I said, it's my problem and not yours, and you have already been kindness itself to me. It is just, well, my husband and your father held similar views."

Shock jolted through Penelope.

This was dangerous territory. Her mother had been very clear with her daughters—never speak of their father's religious or political leanings, not even lightly. It had been all her mother could do to keep them in Polite Society after her father's death. Any whiff of that same scandal and they'd go down in its flames.

"We don't have to speak of them," said Lady Spencer, seeming to sense Penelope's tension. "It is just so comforting to have someone to talk to. I have been out of English Society for so long, and my friends are now strangers to me."

A little of the anxiousness bled away and empathy grew in its place.

"Now you have me," said Penelope with feeling.

"Thank you. If only he would... stop..." Lady Spencer's words hung in the air for Penelope to conjure up her own dramatic ending.

"Is there anything I can do?" she asked.

"Not unless you are very rich." Lady Spencer chuckled, the bitter tone marring her beauty. "The Count he... he has some information about my late husband's... allegiances... dangerous allegiances. You might understand. They could be very damaging even if I am nothing to do with them."

Penelope understood. She had grown up under the threat of similar revelations, and her mother had always told her to avoid any discussions about such topics. Was Lady Spencer really facing those self-same menaces?

"He demands money or my hand."

"The scoundrel!" Penelope exclaimed, her questions eclipsed by sudden indignation. "You should give him neither."

Another mirthless chuckle from the widow. "If only it were that simple—or I had your bravery, Lady Penelope. But alas, I fear I must find the finances he seeks, or I will be shackled to that man forever."

Turning around at this point, they began to retrace their steps.

Righteous indignation burned through Penelope. For the man to hold such power over this woman by these reprehensible threats was detestable. No one should be threatened and certainly not over the sins of their family.

"I shall help you find the money."

"What?" Lady Spencer half-laughed, but Penelope pulled her to a stop and faced her, blue eyes bright and earnest.

"I am perfectly serious. I shall help you."

"But I am a stranger to you—and how could you ever—"

"I will help you," Penelope repeated firmly.

"May I be of service?"

The male voice caused both women to jump and turn towards the gentleman whom neither had seen approaching.

He bowed before Penelope could catch sight of his face. As he rose, Penelope locked eyes with a measuring hazel gaze, and realised disconcertingly that it was Lord Standon.

CHAPTER 4

Roderick really should have been more of a gentleman and not interrupted, but he couldn't seem to help himself after the fascinating encounter the previous evening.

He repeated his offer. "I do not like to interrupt, but if I can be of service?"

It took a moment for the spark of recognition to light in Lady Penelope's eyes, and it evolved quickly into fiery vexation.

"You!"

"'Tis I." Roderick swept another bow and rose with a smile.

Lady Spencer had been at the ball last evening. Roderick had been introduced to her and that Italian fellow who'd been in her company. Was this who Lady Penelope had been ferrying through secret doors?

Lady Spencer inclined her head and gave a practised smile. "Lord Standon."

She was an attractive woman, but one whose freshness of face had disappeared with time. Her elegance and features were enhanced with the artifices common to those who had been out in Society a while. Powder and rouge hid imperfections. Her masked countenance hid her real emotions. It was not that she wasn't beautiful. She was. But the contrast to the innocence of the young Lady Penelope was stark. The Harwood girl's emotions were writ large on her face.

She was *not* happy with Roderick's interruption.

"How kind of you to offer," Lady Spencer continued smoothly. "Have you met my friend? Lady Penelope Harwood, may I present, Lord Standon."

He bowed low again. "A pleasure. I believe we met briefly at the Arleighs' ball?"

Her bright blue eyes narrowed, but she said nothing. This game of cat and mouse was amusing.

"It is a pleasure to be able to acquaint you then. Lady Penelope is a sweet friend of mine. One of the few after such a long sojourn away from England."

"Oh yes," Roderick replied, ignoring the glares from the sweet friend in question. "Italy, wasn't it?"

That was where the Old Pretender had set up his court in exile and his son, Charles Edward Stuart, had become a notable member of Rome society. It came back to Roderick then—hadn't Viscount Spencer married a young miss when in his dotage and taken her off to the Continent?

"That's right."

Roderick noted a challenge in Lady Spencer's green eyes. Yes, that was it—Spencer had been a Jacobite sympathiser right to his grave. No doubt his exile to Italy with his young bride had been driven by a desire to be at the court of the Jacobite Pretender. What was the Harwood girl doing consorting with someone connected to the Stuart heir with her family's past?

Surely the young woman did not realise.

"But it is time for me to leave," Lady Spencer said in a tone that suggested her absence was a reason for mourning. "And while your offer is kind, Lord Standon, my problems are nothing of consequence. Only female matters. Please do not concern yourself."

Lady Penelope made to say something, but Lady Spencer was quick to press her hands and lean forward to whisper in the young woman's ear. Then the older woman pulled back, reiterating what a dear, sweet friend Lady Penelope was, before turning on her heel and gliding off in the direction of her waiting maid.

Roderick watched her go, and then turned back to the abandoned Lady Penelope, very aware of the impropriety of Lady Spencer leaving the young woman alone in a public area.

"May I escort you back to the party you arrived with, Lady Penelope?"

"I suppose," she said, still looking after Lady Spencer.

"Your honesty is refreshing—if a little cutting," Roderick said, half-smiling at the distracted miss. Never had his offer of escort been received with so little fervour.

"What?" she replied in an unladylike way. "I mean, I beg your pardon, my Lord?"

"Do not worry yourself."

He offered his arm, and after a moment of looking off into the middle distance, she took it. Indicating the direction of her mother and sister, they set off.

"I must apologise for interrupting your tête-à-tête with your friend. I gather it is now twice that I have done so."

"Twice?" Her voice was far too high.

"Yes. Once when you appeared to be talking to a portrait, but in actuality were speaking to Lady Spencer through a hidden door. The second time this morning. Tell me—was her secret escape last night linked to the troubles she spoke of just now?"

"You are very forward, my Lord," Lady Penelope blustered.

"Intrigued," he corrected. "Very intrigued. After all, it is not every day a woman pretends that speaking to a painting is clarifying for the mind. Of course, I now know that was nonsense."

"Not necessarily. Don't you speak to yourself sometimes?"

Roderick laughed. This girl was quick-witted. He turned the conversation back to the matter he wished to understand.

"I did mean it, though—my offer of help."

Lady Penelope looked over at him as they continued to walk and he returned her gaze, his own steady.

"I don't even know you."

"You don't know Lady Spencer," Roderick reasoned. "She has only recently come to London."

"You are very interested in my affairs, my Lord. And Lady Spencer's, for that matter."

For such a young woman, Lady Penelope was proving remarkably self-possessed. Had Roderick misjudged her naivety? He could not tell.

"After living with her husband in Italy these past five years or more, I am surprised she has chosen to return to London." Perhaps if he spoke about the widow generally, Lady Penelope might divulge more.

He felt her hand tense on his arm. Was it at his knowledge of her new friend? Or was she cognisant of the connection between Lady Spencer and her own father's scandals?

"That surprises you? I should think it makes perfect sense, given her husband's death. Her closest family is in England."

"You have the advantage of me in sound reasoning," Roderick conceded. "Am I to accept, then, that I may be of no service to you, or Lady Spencer?"

"You are doing a fine service in escorting me back to my Mama and sister." She raised a hand to wave at the ladies in question, who sat on a bench up ahead. "But no, I do not think you can help."

Remarkable.

Most simpering misses would have leapt with open, slathering jaws at such a juicy offer from one of Society's eligible bachelors. Lady Penelope, however, was more zealous over keeping her new friend's confidence than latching onto an marriageable noble's attention.

"May I perhaps, then, offer a little advice?" He could not, as a gentleman, say nothing of the concern he had for the young Harwood's liaison with Lady Spencer. He awaited no confirmation. "Given your family's... ah... history, I believe it may be prudent of you to take care with Lady Spencer. Your heart is all kindness, but her Ladyship is known to—"

"I won't listen to any more of this sermon," Lady Penelope said snatching her hand from his arm and turning to face him.

"I suppose you're obliquely referencing my late father's sympathies?" Again, her directness took Roderick by surprise. "You must think me a wet goose indeed, if you feel the need to speak to me with such euphemisms. I am aware of who my father was. Though I confess I find it shocking indeed—after so short an acquaintance—you feel in any position to lecture me on my family's reputation, or who I choose to befriend, for that matter."

She was getting heated now, her blue eyes blazing, and a flush in those smooth cheeks. Roderick leant on his back foot, wishing he had said nothing, and that there was some way of quenching the fire of her indignation. He opted for the safety of silence.

"It's not the first time a person has taken it upon themselves to speak to me of my father through *good intentions*," she said sarcastically. "Let me be clear, Lord Standon. My father's convictions may not have made sense to me, but he was my father. I had no choice in the matter of being his daughter, and besides, I loved him. I should therefore be a poor woman indeed if I were to judge another for the company their husband kept—or worse—refuse aid for those self-same reasons."

"Lady Penelope, I—"

"No, please." She put up a hand to stop him. "I thank you for your escort, but I don't wish to speak further on the matter. Good day to you, Lord Standon."

She swivelled on her heel and marched away to her waiting mother and sister.

He stood frozen in stunned silence, watching after the small, fierce woman, torn between admiration and indignation. He quickly replayed his actions in his mind. Had he been too forthright? Was his advice deserving of such censure? He had only wished to help. Clearly, she did not need it.

Very well. He had stuck his nose into the affairs of a young lady—something he ordinarily avoided—and his reward was a verbal thrashing.

Unfreezing, he struck out for the main thoroughfare of Rotten Row and left the shocking happenstance behind him. That was the last time he would offer to help the young Lady Penelope.

CHAPTER 5

The only thing Roderick disliked more than the London Season was being locked up on a country estate with the self-same people for a house party. Sir Tristan had invited Lord and Lady Etheridge and their children to just such an event, and his parents had accepted.

With his brother serving in His Majesty's army overseas, and his sister Matilda's recent engagement to a marquess resulting in a stay with her soon-to-be in-laws, it was Roderick and his younger sister Isabel who represented the Etheridge brood. His mother had insisted, and Roderick had begrudgingly acquiesced, having already cried off two balls and another house party invitation. His parents really were desperate to ensure every opportunity for their son and heir to make a match.

Opting to ride, to save himself the monotony of his father's sermonising in the carriage, Roderick had enjoyed the exercise. He loved his parent, but Lord Etheridge could go on about family duty for hours, and Roderick was already well aware his father expected him to find a suitable bride and settle down to the task of procreating in the next year.

They arrived at Sir Tristan's country estate a little after noon the following Friday, and were greeted by their hosts in the great hall of the old Elizabethan manor house.

"Welcome, my boy," said Sir Tristan in his genial way.

Although the man was only a baronet, he had won over many in Society thanks to his winning disposition and philanthropic wife. The possession of an exceedingly large fortune had not done him any harm either.

"Pleasure to have you, my Lord." He grasped Roderick's hand warmly. "I hope to provide you with some excellent shooting while you're here."

"Very kind of you."

Ordinarily, the origins of the Belvedores' wealth being from investments in road building and turnpike trusts across Surrey, rather than from their small estate, would be looked down upon by the ton. But, thought Roderick cynically, the ton could be blind when they wanted to be. A fortune of twenty thousand pounds made them very blind indeed.

"And you, Lady Isabel." Sir Tristan turned his smiling countenance on Roderick's sister and bowed. "My dear wife has planned a picnic by the lake and a bit of boating, if it should take your fancy."

"Oh, how lovely. Yes, please," cried Isabel, clapping her hands together and causing her to appear a child again despite her seventeen years.

Roderick didn't need blinding by the Belvedores' fortune to see them as the kind and congenial hosts they always were.

Lady Belvedore came next, clasping Isabel's hands with the intimacy of an aunt. "My dear Lady Isabel, I am so pleased you could come. I hope some of my other young guests might provide you with good company while you're here. I selected a few, especially for you."

Roderick took a step back to allow his parents to chatter away to Sir Tristan. They proceeded to give an hour-by-hour account of their journey and the roads which, according to their avid analysis, were much better now the turnpike trust was in place. Beside them, Isabel was answering Lady Belvedore's questions about her new dress with glee.

Roderick felt a slight dampening of his spirits. He knew this stay would be more duty than amusement. But the reality sinking in was less than pleasant. Any friends of his were back in London, and while he loved his family and liked his hosts, he feared he was doomed to a tedious visit.

He smiled politely when Lady Belvedore mentioned his name and both she and his sister looked over at him. Then his gaze drifted off again. What would Pendleton and Wedmore be up to in Town? His friends were of the sporting lot and no doubt were at their fencing club, working up a sweat in their daily sparring session. Perhaps he might slope off early and join them after a few days.

Roderick's gaze was now on the end of the hall, not taking much in, when it was suddenly interrupted. Several figures appeared through one of the connecting doors. He focused on a middle-aged woman and two others—younger—perhaps daughters.

The firm line of his mouth faltered. One of those young women was Lady Penelope. What was she doing here? Surely his parents had not known the Harwoods would be in attendance. His father would be most displeased.

The newcomers were advancing on the party in the hall.

"Ah! Here are some of our other guests."

Those clear, expressive blue eyes ran over the faces present, catching on Roderick. Lady Penelope's lips parted. Did she just mouth something? Whatever it was, in the next second she snapped her mouth shut, and a deep furrow appeared across her brow.

So, she was happy to see him then.

"Lord and Lady Etheridge, may I present Lady Harwood and her daughters?"

Roderick's father blustered something, the words catching in his throat, and proceeded to have a mild coughing fit.

"We are acquainted," Lady Harwood said, inclining her head rather than curtseying.

"Ah, splendid, splendid!" said Sir Tristan, apparently immune to the tension. He stepped back to allow Lady Harwood entrance to the gathering. "We invited Lady Penelope and Lady Thalia as a complement to you Isabel. They have already met our other guests."

Unfortunately for Lady Penelope, she was on the side closest to Roderick. She was doing her utmost to keep away from him, as if he might infect her with the plague.

"It's been too long, Athena," Lady Etheridge said, coming to the rescue of her husband's incivility. She stepped forward and held out her hands.

After a concerning pause, Lady Harwood took them, and his mother smiled in her kind way.

"Yes, not since my husband and I hosted a ball in the autumn of 1730. I don't believe I saw you at his funeral." Lady Harwood's cold gaze looked over at Lord Etheridge to whom the statement seemed to be addressed.

"Quite, quite," his father blustered.

"We were so sorry to hear of your loss," said Lady Etheridge, squeezing her old friend's hands and smiling gently. "And so very sad for your girls. But I see they have grown into two beautiful young ladies."

"Absolutely," Sir Tristan said. "With Lady Isabel, Lady Penelope, Lady Thalia *and* Lady Spencer, I declare we gentlemen shall be overcome with beauty."

Isabel giggled and blushed in a becoming manner.

Lady Spencer? Roderick frowned.

How had the widow wangled an invitation to this gathering after such a short time in London?

No. Roderick commanded himself to stop right there. Hadn't he sworn off giving any more advice to the young Harwood woman after she had bitten his head off?

Unfortunately for him, as the ice was now broken across the party and separate conversations were springing up, he found himself paired off with Lady Penelope. No mention of Lady Spencer. No mention of her father. Keep it civil.

"I trust you had a good journey?"

"Thank you, Lord Standon, but I am quite happy to stand in silence. You need not feel obligated to converse with me."

Keeping it light and civil was clearly off the table.

"Very well."

They stood in painful silence for several minutes, Roderick trying to avoid anyone else's gaze, should they notice the atmosphere between himself and the elder Harwood girl.

"Roderick's a great rider."

His ears pricked up at his sister's words.

"Aren't you, brother? He rode all the way here." Isabel was speaking to Lady Thalia. "I'm sure he could give your Lord Fairing a gallop for his money."

"Lord Fairing is a very accomplished rider," Lady Thalia replied earnestly. "N-not that I mean you are n-not, my Lord." Her expression transformed to one of anxiety.

"Do not fear, Lady Thalia," said Roderick kindly, "I happen to know Fairing is an excellent horseman. I am happy to acknowledge his prowess."

"Why didn't you come in your family's carriage?" asked Lady Penelope. "It's a long way from London, even for an experienced rider. Didn't you wish to spare your horse?"

Roderick turned his gaze upon her. The lady was willing to converse—but only when she could point out fault.

"My brother cannot abide too much chatter on long journeys," Isabel said, answering on his behalf. "He will not travel in the carriage unless everyone promises they will be silent for at least a part of the journey. Papa will do no such thing." His sister started giggling.

"Lord Standon sounds like you, Pen." Lady Thalia poked her older sister, grinning in such a way as to produce an eye roll from the recipient.

"Nonsense," Lady Penelope replied. "I didn't ride here."

"No, but you did demand that Mama and I stop talking halfway here so that you might concentrate on your thoughts and admire the view outside the window. Whoever heard of someone needing silence to look at a view?"

Isabel and Lady Thalia unleashed a cacophony of giggles. Their sudden alliance was concerning. There was nothing as troublesome as two young women armed with camaraderie and wit.

Lady Penelope rolled her eyes again. "I should like to have ridden here *now* if it would have spared me from this ridicule," she said, huffing. "Though I see you are a little worse for wear for your independence." Her eyes ran up and down Roderick's frame, settling on his mud-spattered boots and breeches.

"I can only apologise for my poor state." He offered a mocking bow.

Lady Penelope chose not to acknowledge it. "I would take a little mud on my skirts if it would stop these two."

An involuntarily chuckle rumbled through Roderick's chest. One moment she was a prickly thistle. The next her sharp wit had him laughing.

"You echo my sentiments exactly."

Perhaps they might enjoy a truce after all.

"I haven't met her yet—my sister has," Isabel was saying to Lady Thalia. "Do you know Lady Spencer, Roderick?" She turned from her new-found confidant to look expectantly at her brother. "Is she as pretty as they say?"

"I have met her," Roderick replied, feeling Lady Penelope's eyes hard upon him.

"He does not speak of her beauty." Isabel was giggling again. "You know what that means." She and Lady Thalia fell to whispering.

Roderick left the two young women to their intrigues and decided to build on the fragile peace with Lady Penelope. "Perhaps we are not so different after all, if our travelling preferences are anything to go by." He hoped it sounded like the olive branch he intended.

"I don't think so," the lady replied without hesitation. "I hear your disapproval of Lady Spencer in your tone. At least on that count we are at odds."

He bristled. "You give your opinion very readily, Lady Penelope."

"I could well say the same of you."

"I only hoped we might find common ground. We need not be at dagger drawing. I may have given unsolicited advice on your friendship with a certain widow, but that does not mean—"

"Thank goodness I do not hold your advice in high regard."

Very well, if she traded in frankness, frank he would be.

"I should have paid heed to your first words and maintained my silence. Any attempt at civility is in vain if it is only to be received with rudeness." He was going to carry on, but she cut across his thought.

"Yes." The fire in her voice was dampened. "I am being dreadfully rude."

Roderick's brows shot up. This woman was one candid surprise after another.

"I apologise. You are trying very hard to be polite—I can see that—it's just that now I have seen *him*... I am so worried for... Oh, no! Ignore me. I will not use that as an excuse." She turned to face him, her blue eyes all earnestness. "I beg your pardon, Lord Standon. I was too quick to assume another sermon from you."

"I can hardly keep up with you, Lady Penelope, you travel at such a pace."

"I know," she replied ruefully, humour hovering about her lips. "Mother says I go abominably fast."

Roderick could not agree more wholeheartedly with Lady Harwood's estimation of her elder daughter. This young woman before him was bewildering. She was neither a naive, fresh from the schoolroom miss, nor was she entirely worldly-wise. She bounced between the two states with a stubbornness underpinning the whole.

"Shall I draw up my sword, and you yours?" she asked.

Roderick resisted the urge to state the obvious—that his weapon had never been drawn. "I should like that."

Lady Penelope nodded in a business-like fashion and they fell into amicable silence.

After a time, the hosts finished their welcomes and encouraged their new arrivals up the stairs to rest after their journey.

Roderick needed no second bidding. His fears this would be a dull house party were fast evaporating. Replacing them was a growing concern that this gathering would be anything but dull.

He followed a servant upstairs and along the passage leading to the east wing. At that moment, a gentleman with dark features came around the corner at the far end. He strode towards Roderick and the servant, forcing them to give way, and barely offering an acknowledgement as he did so.

He wore a blue silk suit, the stiff skirts of which were far wider than the English styles, and the smell of pipe smoke emanating from him was overpowering. Was this Feccio?

Roderick caught the glitter of diamonds from his shoe

buckles, and then the flash of a ring—a sapphire? No, there was white at its centre. A flower. Then it was gone, along with its wearer, down the hall and thence down the stairs of the manor.

"Who was that gentleman?" asked Roderick.

"Count Feccio, my Lord."

It *was* him.

"This way, my Lord," said the servant, resuming his walk along the passageway.

Roderick followed, not listening to the description of the room he was to stay in, nor where the bell was to call for a servant.

His mind was in quite another place. Since trying to warn Lady Penelope away from friendship with Lady Spencer in Hyde Park, Roderick had concluded that perhaps he had over-reacted. He should not judge Lady Spencer by the affiliations of her dead husband. That headstrong Harwood woman had a point on that count. Since that day on Rotten Row, he had supposed there really was nothing more to their sudden attachment than a female kinship.

But that was before Roderick had seen Count Feccio's ring.

That white flower he had seen was a rose. A white rose on a bed of blue. There was no mistaking the symbolism of that ring. It declared loyalty to an exiled king. There were Jacobites under Sir Tristan's roof.

Roderick and Lady Penelope had only just called a truce, but he now had the distinctly uncomfortable feeling he was going to have to break it.

CHAPTER 6

Sir Tristan and Lady Belvedore had arranged a picnic by the lake for the following day. About mid-morning a procession of open-topped carriages with finely clad passengers made their leisurely way down the avenues of trees towards the water. The excited chatter, particularly among the younger members of the party, only increased when rumours began circulating that Sir Tristan had ordered rowboats to be brought from the boathouse.

Despite being horrified on Lady Spencer's behalf that Count Feccio had secured an invitation to the same house party, Penelope couldn't help getting caught up in a little of the excitement. She had only been on a rowboat once before. It had been when her father was alive. He had taken her and Thalia on the river in Oxford.

It was only a short drive across the estate, and the carriages halted in a synchronised fashion at the site of a Turkish tent pitched at the water's edge. The sides of the majestic blue and white structure were swept open to reveal tables piled high with food, surrounded by chairs, blankets and a scattering of rugs.

"It's magical!" Thalia exclaimed.

The weather was with them, the sun sparkling across the water. As if on cue, a family of swans launched onto the lake as they arrived, floating into view through the opening of the tent and completing the idyllic picture.

"He's doing it again," Thalia whispered to Penelope. "Lord Standon—he's staring."

A prickling sensation crept up the back of Penelope's neck. "No, he isn't."

"You didn't even look. I can see him plain as day from here."

Penelope rolled her eyes and, determined to prove her sister wrong, turned around to observe the Etheridges' carriage. "There, you see. He does not look this way at all."

"He *was*," Thalia returned. "*And* he was doing it this morning at breakfast. I should like Lord Fairing to stare at me as intently as Lord Standon does you." Her sister was giggling abominably now. She had struck gold finding this nerve of Penelope's and would keep prodding it as long as it gained a reaction.

"Oh, do be quiet!" Penelope snapped, heat now accompanying the prickling sensation. "He does no such thing. In fact, I'm certain he doesn't like me."

"What makes you say that?" asked Lady Harwood, who had hitherto been ignoring her bickering daughters.

"Oh, um—" Penelope waved a hand, not wishing to admit how rude she had been to Lord Standon. "I just think he is likely used to dull-witted chits with no opinions."

Lady Harwood gave her elder daughter a hard look. "I may have raised you to have a mind—and educated you beyond what most girls experience—but I hope I did not breed rudeness?"

"No, Mama." Penelope bowed her head. She could hardly

explain why she was at odds with Lord Standon. "It is just that he mentioned Father."

"I see. Well, I believe I've taught you, have I not, that we do not need to add any fuel to the fire when Society already thinks so poorly of us?"

"Yes, you have. It's just—" Penelope changed tack. "I saw how Lord Etheridge was with you."

"That? Oh, well, I saw no harm in highlighting the fact that the Etheridges have snubbed us since your father's death. I was once quite close friends with Lady Etheridge. But unlike you two, I do not have marriages to think about. What have I taught you to do when anyone insensitively mentions your father's religious and political leanings?"

"I raise my head high, say nothing, and remember that Society has a way of being inexplicably stupid sometimes."

Thalia was giggling again.

"Precisely."

"But Mama, is *that* not rude?" asked Thalia, still laughing.

"One does not say it to people's faces, my dear—now stop that or you'll have one of your coughing fits."

At that moment, Thalia began spluttering, descending into a racking cough as the driver let down the steps. Penelope and her mother waited until her sister's upset eased and then descended from the carriage.

There was a general melee as the vehicles released their occupants and servants rushed around holding out parasols and carrying shawls. Penelope found it easy enough to slip away from her family and find her way to Lady Spencer's side.

"How are you this morning?" Penelope whispered to her new friend.

Lady Spencer had just commented on the size of the lake and Sir Tristan was explaining he had recently stocked the body of water with fish. His audience included Lord and Lady

Etheridge and Count Feccio, so Lady Spencer was able to turn away with Penelope after a few minutes.

"Oh, thank you, thank you! I wasn't sure how much longer I could bear to be in the Count's company."

"I couldn't believe it when you were put in a carriage with him."

"Oh yes, Lady Penelope," Lady Spencer said, loud enough for the others to hear. "The boats look so delightful. Let us go and inspect the vessels so we may choose our favourite for later."

Taking Penelope's arm, she guided her away from the others, towards a little jetty at the edge of the lake.

"But what is he even doing here?" Penelope continued once they were safely out of earshot. "I didn't know Sir Tristan and Lady Belvedore were acquainted with him. He is so new to London."

"It is the ill-fortune of my life." Her Ladyship sighed.

Being taller, her strides were longer than Penelope's, and the emerald-green *robe volante* she wore flared dramatically, adding expression to her words. Penelope found herself admiring the matching silk mules and artfully placed bergère hat that completed her Ladyship's ensemble. Even aggravated she appeared elegance personified.

"I was so thrilled to procure an invitation to this house party—for I knew you were invited and I planned to know you better—only to find that insidious man has followed me." She threw one hand up into the air, the lace *engageates* decorating the elbows of her wide sleeve fluttering as she did so.

"I don't understand. Never mind how he got the invitation—how did he even know you were going to be here?"

"Ah!" Lady Spencer looked away into the middle distance, dropping her pretty little parasol onto her shoulder, its tassels bobbing. "I hardly know how he does it."

"But there must have been—"

"How am I to know?" Lady Spencer snapped, eyes flashing with sudden irritation. "It's distressing enough to find him here. Am I also to be interrogated?"

"Oh, no! That's not—I did not mean—" Heat flooded Penelope's cheeks, her step faltering.

"There now." Lady Spencer's voice reverted to one of softness. "You are such a sweet child. You don't know the wiles that men use to get what they want."

Penelope bristled a little at the condescending tone, but swallowed her pride. "I will speak no more of how he got here. I am only sorry for it."

"And I—the things he has threatened... they are vile, Lady Penelope, vile."

"I have asked for an advance on my pin money, and my mother has agreed. Will that help?"

"So very sweet of you, my child."

Penelope ground her teeth against the endearment. She *wasn't* a child.

"I—" Lady Spencer stopped at the water's edge and fiddled with the bone handle of her parasol, causing it to spin in a dizzying fashion. Her eyes appeared to fill with tears, though none tracked down her face to spoil the carefully applied powder and rouge. "I had hoped it would help, but he has now asked for more. He says..." She trailed off.

"Surely it cannot be worse?" Penelope saw the distress on Lady Spencer's face and, realising how petty her feelings were, she pushed the frustration away. Her new friend needed help.

"So much worse," the widow breathed, her voice barely audible. "He says he will expose me for my—my political leanings. He is accusing me of..." Lady Spencer's eyes flicked to the lake, then to Penelope, sharp and penetrating. Penelope's blood ran cold.

"Given who your father was, I feel I can tell you. Feccio says he will ensure everyone of consequence in Society knows it was not just my husband who supported the Stuart cause. He will say I am a secret Catholic. That I supported the Stuart cause as well—and that I still do."

Even knowing it was coming, the words still dashed over Penelope like ice cold water.

"He even insinuated that my knowing you would seal my fate in Society's eyes. And that... that fraternising with a Harwood means I know one who harbours the Old Pretender's treasure."

Treasure? The mention of that infamous treasure hit Penelope hard. How long had it been since she had heard that damaging rumour bandied about?

"It is no doubt his way of forcing me to accept his hand. That and tripling the amount for my release."

"Tripling?" Penelope gasped. "The scoundrel." She did not respond to the mention of the Old Pretender's treasure. Her mother had told her not to feed such rumours. "You must take my pin money. It has to be better than nothing, and it may stave him off for a little longer."

"Are you sure? I can call on you when we return to London."

"Positively. I should have it from Mama when I get back. In the meantime, you may stay in my company as much as you need while we're here to avoid that odious man."

"How can I ever thank you? You are the sweetest of girls." And then, without missing a breath, she said, "Now, let's rejoin the party before we are missed—there is surely still fun to be had while we're here."

With a suddenness that left Penelope's mind spinning, Lady Spencer seemed to recover from her fears. The widow dragged her back to the party. Within minutes Lady Spencer was the most amusing of companions and no one could have guessed anything was amiss.

CHAPTER 7

Despite Penelope's best attempts, Count Feccio managed to weasel his way into a rowboat with Lady Spencer and the Etheridge daughter after the picnic.

She mouthed an apology to the widow before turning back with a somewhat sour face to Thalia who was doing her best performance of a tragedienne.

"I should have loved to have been in a boat with Lord Fairing. I expect he is an exceptionally strong rower."

"Oh, do stop going on about him," Penelope begged, looping her arm through her sister's and dragging them towards one of the remaining boats on the jetty.

"I can't help it," her sister replied.

Penelope softened a little. If they set off quickly, she might be able to keep an eye on the Count.

"Come now, we shall have fun on the lake, even without your dear Lord Fairing." She squeezed her sister's arm affectionately.

There were two servants waiting to hand them into one of the boats and hold the vessel steady. Thalia squealed when the boat they chose moved under her foot. She fell with a thump onto the seat and altered the subject of her moaning. "I shan't be rowing, Pen. You know how Mama is always telling me to preserve my strength."

Penelope frowned, huffing as she stepped down into the boat. "What makes you think I can do it all?"

"Ready to cast off, my Lady?" one of the servants asked Penelope, holding the boat's mooring rope in his hand.

"Woah there! Hold, my good man," came a call from along the jetty.

Penelope and Thalia turned to see Lord Standon striding behind one of the servants.

"Good afternoon, ladies. Perhaps I may be of service and take on the role of your rower?"

"Oh, that would be splendid!" said Thalia before Penelope could think of a polite excuse.

She may have made peace with the man, but that didn't mean she wished to go boating with him.

Before she could respond, however, Lord Standon climbed down into the vessel, took the mooring rope from the servant, and was settled into his seat.

He pushed off and she watched with begrudging admiration as he took up the oars and began pulling them with long, strong strokes, propelling the little craft and its occupants out onto the lake.

"I suspect he might be as good a rower as Lord Fairing would be," Thalia whispered.

Penelope rolled her eyes and turned her gaze to the changing view of the water and lakeside.

"And how," Lord Standon asked between powerful strokes, "have you both been enjoying the picnic thus far?"

"Very much, thank you, Lord Standon." Thalia beamed at him, thrilled she was not required to exert any physical effort for this excursion. "I was so pleased when I saw Lady Belvedore had iced buns with jam on the table. And sweetmeats and strawberry cordial."

While her sister chattered on in this fashion, Penelope occupied herself by spying on the other vessels in the distance. Not that she could be of any help to Lady Spencer out here. She could see Count Feccio rowing sedately, and her Ladyship leant back smiling and conversing with him as though they were old friends. Penelope hardly knew how she maintained such civility given the circumstances.

"And you, Lady Penelope—are you equally delighted by the repast our hosts are treating us to?"

Drawn reluctantly from her observations, Penelope's gaze fell on Lord Standon. She was a little perturbed by the directness of those hazel eyes. Her stomach did an unauthorised flutter.

"I do not have such a sweet tooth as my sister," she replied, finding it very vexing that her heart was being as rebellious as her stomach. How it did race! "But I am partial to those raspberry jellies I saw. And yourself, my Lord?"

"The roast beef and Sir Tristan's cider for me." He grinned, and Penelope couldn't deny the handsomeness of that face. He had the sort of eyes that looked made for smiling.

"Oh, look—fish!" Thalia cried, pointing a gloved finger over the side of the boat.

All three occupants moved instinctively to see, and the boat lurched to the right.

Penelope, nearest that side, squealed, clutching at the boat only to find air. She careened towards the dipped side of the vessel and felt sure she would fall into the water when a strong arm encircled her waist and pulled her back into the boat's centre.

"Gracious!" Thalia screeched, a hand on either side of the boat to maintain her balance.

"The perils of a rowboat," said Lord Standon, chuckling in Penelope's ear.

She could feel his strong frame behind her, the rise of his chest, and the weight of his arm across her bodice. Heat flooded up her neck, and that traitorous stomach of hers danced and flipped within her.

Thalia, who had barely attended the trials of the couple at the other end of the boat, cried out once more. "There are more of them." She pointed again to the water.

"Take care, Lady Thalia, or your nature-watching shall send us all overboard."

"There are so many. I think they must be trout."

"You great goose!" Penelope snapped.

Thalia paid no heed.

"You and I had better stay where we are while your sister enjoys the fish," said Lord Standon, still with his arm around her waist.

Penelope simply *could not* stay where she was. Lord Standon was practically embracing her. Pulling free, she turned on her seat to face him.

"Are you all right?" He leant forward and Penelope was assailed by the scent of amber and vanilla. "That was quite a fright."

He seemed genuinely concerned. She managed a small smile as the heat in her cheeks ebbed.

"Yes, I am only sorry that my sister is so silly."

Lord Standon's face broke into a grin and he chuckled. She observed his arms, and the large hands carelessly clasped between his legs. She had been in those arms a moment ago... There it went again—her stomach, being traitorous.

Thalia giggled at the far end of the boat, dipping bare fingers in the water as the fish played in the sun just below the surface.

"We could be drowning in the lake for all she cares," Penelope said, half-peevishly, half-ruefully.

"I have no intention of letting any of us drown while I have charge of this boat. And besides, being drowned would put a distinct damper on the rest of the day."

Was he being... amusing?

"Though perhaps a light drowning of one of us would benefit me. Now I know you do not possess a sweet tooth, you will be a rival for all the savoury items on offer."

Penelope giggled. She giggled! How dreadfully embarrassing that she was being won over by his flirting.

"Are you suggesting you might throw me overboard in order to get your hands on Sir Tristan's roast beef?"

"I should never confirm such a dastardly plan." The corner of his mouth quirked up in a roguishly handsome fashion.

Penelope rolled her eyes, determined not to laugh again. She needed her stomach to behave. There were more important things to concentrate on and besides, she was trying to keep this man at arm's length. After all, he'd made his opinions of her family very clear.

She stared out across the lake, hoping it might stop this flirtatious conversation. Lady Spencer's boat was off to the left and Penelope's own vessel was starting to drift around a natural bend in the oxbow lake. It would soon take them out of view.

"I was surprised to see Count Feccio in attendance," Lord Standon said, the funning tone gone.

Penelope's head snapped round. He had followed her gaze.

"It appears that he and Lady Spencer are old acquaintances." He spoke low enough that Thalia would not hear.

"Appearances can be deceiving," Penelope replied in a challenging tone.

But as she looked back at the couple across the lake, she

realised from here they really did look like old friends. The sound of Lady Spencer's laughter carried across the water.

"The Count wears a white rose on his signet ring," Lord Standon said without preamble.

Penelope's eyes widened and her lips parted a fraction. The rose was an undeniable Jacobite symbol. It made sense then, that the Count should be blackmailing Lady Spencer over her husband's affiliations with the exiled court. Who better to know of them? And she was no doubt attempting to misdirect his ire with her friendly attitude in that boat.

"I thought we had agreed you wouldn't interfere in my friendship with Lady Spencer." Penelope's tone was ice. "Am I to think your word as a gentleman is no good, or are you tasked by His Majesty's government to search out Jacobite spies and suspect me to be one?"

She was quite pleased with herself for such a quick-witted rejoinder.

"Neither," Lord Standon replied calmly, his gaze steady upon her. "Merely a concerned bystander. You have already told me you do not share your late father's views. I have no reason to doubt you. But I fear you are moving in dangerous circles and do not realise."

"When will everyone stop treating me like a child?" Penelope snapped. "You, my Lord, underestimate me. I have grown up in the shadow of scandal, so I am not so innocent of the world as you seem to suppose. But perhaps it is because of my childhood I have more feeling for others who suffer under the same scrutiny."

If she wasn't so preoccupied with setting Lord Standon down, Penelope might have realised that Thalia's giggles were fading. Soon her sister might overhear this conversation.

Heart racing, and not for the same reasons as before, Penelope knew her feelings were coming free from her control. Her next words came out too quickly to appear composed and revealed far more than she intended. "And perhaps I owe something to Lady Spencer when her association with me has only added to her troubles."

Lord Standon's brow furrowed. Bother the man! Now he looked more intrigued.

"What blame has she laid at your door?" he asked, an edge to his voice.

"None which I have not laid there myself. Now will you desist from—" Penelope squealed. Someone's long fingers were trailing along her arm. Then across her back. Who was that? She swung round only to realise those living fingers belonged to no insidious interloper, but the reeds.

They were drifting dangerously close to the bank.

"Perhaps if you ceased to be so interested in my affairs and thinking me a dolt incapable of commanding them, we would not be in danger of running aground."

"I think no such thing."

"From Lord Etheridge's reception of my mother, I can see very clearly what your family think of mine. I am only surprised you wish to speak to me at all."

Lord Standon took up the oars which he had drawn into the boat and was setting them in their rowlocks once more. There was a current here, and the boat was picking up speed towards the bank.

"We're veering very close to the lake's edge," called Thalia from the bow.

"Is it so hard to believe," said Lord Standon, struggling to get the oars in the water due to the multiplying reeds, "that I wish to help?"

"I don't need your help!"

As soon as the stubborn words were out of Penelope's mouth, there was the sound of grating, a gentle thud, and they lurched forward as the boat ran aground. The party took a moment to right themselves and absorb their predicament.

And it was in that moment that Penelope realised, in a most infuriating turn of events, that she had ended up in his Lordship's arms once again.

"The reeds are quite thick here," said Lord Standon after Penelope had extricated herself. "You see those mallards nesting? I believe I can get us to shore if we are careful where we step."

"Surely we should just dislodge the boat?" Penelope said, feeling a childish urge to disagree with whatever he said.

"I shouldn't think so," said Thalia, peering over at the reeds and mud surrounding the vessel.

"Better to cut our losses," replied Lord Standon. "Dislodging it will likely cause enough motion to send us all overboard. I should not want to lose my passengers having already run us aground."

"Oh, it was just a mistake," said Thalia, in consoling tones.

Would her sister just hold her tongue! This man needed no encouragement. Penelope picked up one of the oars and tried to find purchase with it on the vegetation.

Telling the sisters to hold on to the sides of the boat, Lord Standon slowly stood up. The stern of the boat was freer than the bow and shifted in the water. Spying a suitable bit of thick reed bed, he carefully stepped out, one foot and then the other. Having found safe ground, he turned back to the boat's occupants.

"If you give me your hand, Lady Thalia, and step just here,"—he pointed—"I shall be able to guide you safely to shore."

"You will ruin your shoes, Thalia. Stay here and I will free us." Penelope started digging into the reeds with the single oar.

"Stop it, Pen!" she screeched in panic. "I just wish to return to the picnic."

Thalia took Lord Standon's offered hand and rose, like a

calf standing for the first time, with shaking legs and uncertain feet.

"That's it—now step here."

Rather than slowly stepping out as his Lordship had done, Thalia practically leapt from the boat. The heavy landing sent her shoes through the reed bed and into the muddy water. She squealed, leaping and prancing as Lord Standon did his best to stop her falling, until eventually she made the solid bank several feet away.

"I told you!" cried Penelope, jamming the oar in harder.

"Lady Penelope—please let me help you."

"Now you are both out I feel the boat moving again—I can get it free—"

At that moment the vessel lurched away from the bank. Penelope was so surprised at the motion, that the oar she held clattered through its holder, and fell out into the reeds. The boat shot off into the lake leaving Lord Standon with hand outstretched, gaping after her.

As soon as she had managed to release the vessel, she knew it was a mistake. The bank receded and the open water swirled around her. Snatching up the remaining oar, she shoved it through the rowlock and began pulling. But it only succeeded in turning her in a circle, getting her no closer to shore.

Well done, Penelope. Now what would she do?

CHAPTER 8

Exasperating woman!

"Oh, no, no, no. She'll drown!" cried Lady Thalia.

Roderick resisted the urge to command the young lady's silence. Her panicking was hardly going to help her headstrong sister, now stranded in the middle of the lake.

Lady Thalia pointed towards her sibling who was furiously rowing with one oar. "Look. She's going around in circles—she'll never get back to shore."

As if caught in a sinister whirlpool, Lady Penelope was swivelling round and round. The faster she rowed for release, the quicker she spun. She was determined. Roderick would give her that.

There was only one thing to be done.

"Lady Thalia, perhaps you might return to your mother and explain what has happened. Order the servants to bring some towels and draw a hot bath at the house."

"You think she will sink."

"No," Roderick replied patiently. He did not need an audience for this rescue and the quicker he could send Lady Thalia off, the quicker he could stop Lady Penelope from making herself dizzy. "She is quite safe, but I expect you would like a towel for your wet feet and a hot bath to warm you up."

She was not the only one who would need a towel and bath after this day was done.

"Indeed I shall. Most thoughtful. Mother will worry I'll catch a cold." The young lady nodded seriously. "I shall go and ask. But—"

She gestured to her stranded sibling.

"Have no fear, Lady Thalia. I shall stay with your sister."

"Of course—yes—I shall go." With one last concerned look towards her sister, she turned on her heel and hurried away around the lake.

Good. One problem dealt with.

Roderick turned back towards the damsel in distress and began unbuttoning his jacket. There was only one way to save Lady Penelope. He removed his outer garment and set to work on his waistcoat before removing his boots and stockings. His cravat and wig went onto the pile of discarded clothes on the bank. It was going to be jolly cold.

Lady Penelope was still rowing vigorously with that oar. Would the woman never give up?

Taking a deep breath, and bracing himself against the chill, he waded into the water. Not wishing to prolong the discomfort, once the water was past his waist, he launched himself into the lake and headed out towards his quarry.

If the water hadn't been quite so cold, and the situation not been quite so frustrating, he might have enjoyed such a swim. The sun was on the water, the ducks were swimming at the lake's edge, and all seemed right with the world.

All, that was, except Lady Penelope, who was thrashing around like a landed fish.

"Ahoy there!" he shouted, stopping short of the radius of the oar she was plunging around like a maniac. "Might you pull in your weapon and spare my skull?"

"Gracious!" she cried, dropping the oar in fright and watching it rattle through the rowlock into the lake.

"Not quite what I meant," said Roderick, swimming towards the oar and grabbing hold of it before it floated off.

"What *are* you doing?"

He towed the oar towards the boat which had slowed its frenzied spin.

"I thought it would be nice to go for a swim. And what are *you* doing, Lady Penelope?" he asked, reaching the boat and throwing the oar over into its bottom, sending a shower of water towards its occupant.

"Urgh!" Lady Penelope cried, blue eyes flashing angrily at him.

She might be infuriating, but goodness was she beautiful when she looked like that. He half-believed she would have managed to row herself to shore eventually with that kind of spirit.

"You are soaked and it's all my fault."

He recognised that expression. Guilt.

"No harm done, particularly to my skull." He took hold of the boat's side and began manoeuvring it, so he was positioned at the bow. "If you would be so good as to throw the mooring rope out, I might tow you to shore."

"You don't have your wig on," she remarked, quite out of kilter with the circumstances. "I should never have guessed you had such jet-black hair."

Roderick started chuckling.

"Well, I shouldn't have," said Lady Penelope frankly, finding the rope and tossing the end overboard.

He couldn't help it, he started laughing. This woman was mad, quite mad.

"You must stop, my Lady. I cannot maintain buoyancy while laughing."

"Oh, sorry." She pressed a forefinger across her closed lips endearingly.

"Right." He took the rope and turned towards the bank. "Now I shall be your sea horse, Lady Penelope." He began swimming, boat and lady in tow.

Before ten minutes had passed, Lady Penelope and her renegade vessel were once again scraping onto the reed beds, and Roderick, with water pouring off him, was clambering out of the shallows. He pulled the vessel securely onto the vegetation and, finding purchase on the reeds, he turned back to hand the rescued maiden out of the boat.

"You did a very rash thing in coming to save me," Penelope scolded.

It was far easier to focus on being cross with the man than acknowledge the transparent wet shirt, soaked breeches and bare calves. "You might catch your death of cold and then I shall be a murderer."

Such spectacular legs!

"If you will do me the favour of taking my hand to shore, I might find some dry clothes and avoid imminent death—and you in turn should avoid the noose, of course. Your hand, if you please."

He was being amusing. How vexing. Ignoring his funning, Penelope shuffled forward on her bench and stood. The boat bobbed, even where it was on the reeds.

"Easy," Lord Standon murmured, eyes on the vessel.

Penelope focused on his face as if it might steady the boat. Water droplets were running from his dark hair, down the plains of his cheeks and along that chiselled jaw. She imagined running her fingers along that jawline. Sudden red-hot colour rushed up her neck and into her cheeks.

"You will be all right if you move slowly."

Could he see her blushing? Yes. He was looking directly at her. This was awful. She only hoped he mistook her attraction for nerves at her dilemma.

Slowing her movement, she edged towards the bow of the boat, and took hold of Lord Standon's strong hand.

"The driest patch is here." He pointed. "We must do our best to save those fine silk mules of yours."

"How can you talk of such a thing when you are dripping wet and half-clothed? Where *are* your clothes?"

"Sacrificed willingly in the name of your safety."

"I did not ask you to save me!" Penelope retorted.

"Step here." He pointed again, and Penelope obediently stepped past him, their figures brushing against each other as she did so. She shivered.

Not wanting to draw attention to any reaction she was having to his Lordship, she quickly made to step again, but found her back foot was stuck. She tugged. Her balance failed. It would not come free.

Squealing, she lurched forward. Lord Standon grabbed her up in his arms, stumbled backwards under her momentum, pulling her with him. He tripped and sent them both careening onto the bank.

A moment later, Penelope raised her head from Lord Standon's chest, trying to gain her bearings. They were on land. She looked down at his Lordship's face. His eyes were closed. Was he injured?

He started to shudder. What had she done to him?

"Lord Standon?" She scrambled to find the ground with one hand and pushed herself up off his chest. "Are you all right, my Lord?" Peering down into his face, hers all concern, she saw the flash of white teeth. The shuddering increased. Then he let out a great roll of laughter.

"Thank goodness!" she cried, relief flooding through her as she pushed off his chest and onto the grass beside him.

She hadn't killed him. Taking a great lungful of air, she cast her eyes heavenwards, and lay still, waiting for her nerves to steady.

"You are a very difficult woman to help, Lady Penelope—do you know that?" said Lord Standon between rolls of laughter.

"I suppose I am." She looked over at the profile of his handsome face, creased with laughter and stripped of formality.

Lord Standon continued to laugh at that admission, wiping his eyes. She left him to his amusement and sat up, feeling a little steadier. Batting away her tangled skirts, she set to examining the wet patches all over her dress. It hadn't penetrated through to her chemise, but she did look a mess.

His laughter finally subsiding, his Lordship sat up beside her, and she took in the green and brown stains all over his clothes, and the reed that stuck out like a feather in his hair.

"Here." She leant over to pluck it out.

Lord Standon stilled, his hazel eyes fixed on her countenance as she leant so close to him they were inches apart.

"I'm obliged," he said when she pulled the reed from his hair and showed it to him. "I find you, Lady Penelope, absolutely fascinating." He did not move away, and neither did she.

Penelope's heart fluttered.

Her lips parted in surprise and she saw his eyes immediately drawn to them.

Was he going to...?

"Infuriating you mean."

"No."

And with that, Lord Standon leant in and brushed his lips against hers so lightly it was like a dream. Tingles ran over her skin, the sensation of pleasure spreading out from her mouth, across her skin and deepening as it reached her stomach.

She emitted a tiny gasp. Or did she? She wasn't breathing. Surely that meant she couldn't gasp?

She wanted him to kiss her again. But he wasn't going to. He had pulled back and his gaze was running all over her face, from her eyes to her cheeks to her lips. He was observing the effect he'd had on her.

Had he enjoyed that kiss? Had he enjoyed making her gasp?

"Hallo!" cried Sir Tristan. Their host headed the rest of the house party who were walking around the lake at the direction of Lady Thalia. "A rescue has been performed!"

Penelope and Lord Standon moved apart immediately. Soon they were descended upon and the fussing of the others precluded further conversation.

Towels were distributed, Lord Standon was praised for his rescue, and Penelope was cared for solicitously by the ladies of the party when they returned to the safety of the Turkish tent. His Lordship went up to the house for a change of clothes, and for the rest of the afternoon Penelope did her best to hide the wet stains across the bodice of her dress.

CHAPTER 9

The kiss she had shared with Lord Standon by the lake meant nothing to him.

Penelope had made this determination when he had been all politeness afterwards, making no attempt to build on his attentions, and had then quit Sir Tristan and Lady Belvedore's party for business in London two days after the picnic.

Was she disappointed?

She wasn't sure why she should be. She had not intended to catch his eye. In fact, he had been a provoking pest for their short acquaintance. And yet...

"Penelope Ariadne Harwood!" she said, scolding herself.

How many times must her traitorous mind replay the kiss by the lakeside?

Thankfully she was in the privacy of her bedroom back in their London home. The house party had been wholly uneventful after the picnic. Lady Spencer and Count Feccio had left earlier than expected, Lord Standon a day after, and only the Harwoods and the rest of the Etheridge family had remained. However civil it had been, Penelope had felt sorry for Sir Tristan and Lady Belvedore dealing with such contrasting guests.

It was quite clear the Etheridges were avoiding too much time spent with Penelope's family. She was sure they went on more walks with their daughter in the remainder of that week than they probably had their whole lives. No doubt avoiding the polluting influence of the Harwood family. Perhaps that was why Lord Standon had run away—realising just who he had chosen to kiss by the lakeside.

Penelope and her family returned to London at the week's end, and Thalia had been thrilled at the prospect of being in the orbit of her beloved Lord Fairing again. This morning the younger Harwood sister had gone with a friend to Twining's tea shop on the Strand in the hopes of bumping into the noble, leaving Penelope and her mother at home.

Fed up of circling around the topic of Lord Standon in her head, Penelope left her room and went in search of her mother.

She found her parent writing up menus with the house-keeper in the study. The sun-soaked room in the south-east side of the Town house had been her father's study when he was alive. She supposed her mother took it over after his death as a way of feeling closer to him.

"We cannot have beef two nights in a row, Mrs Hughes," Lady Harwood said, her quill scratching a firm line through one of the menu sheets. "It will be far too heavy for my girls—let's move both of these to Thursday and Friday, and we may then have fish on the latter."

"Yes, your Ladyship."

"Good morning, Mama," said Penelope, dropping into a chair beside her mother's writing desk.

"Good morning, darling. That will be all for now, Mrs Hughes. Penelope, some tea?"

"Yes, please."

"Mrs Hughes, will you be so good as to bring a tray?"

"Yes, my Lady." The middle-aged retainer bobbed a curtsey and retreated.

Lady Harwood turned back to her desk, dipping her quill in the inkpot and scratching words on several more sheets of paper in silence. After two more sheets were dusted and blotted, she discarded her quill and straightened the pile of papers.

"All menus sorted, Mama?" asked Penelope politely, knowing she was invading her mother's housekeeping time.

Every morning from nine until twelve, apart from receiving callers, Lady Harwood spent her time seeing to the accounts and organising the household. Her work had doubled when Lord Harwood had died. On Thursdays and Fridays, she now oversaw the keeping of the Town house mews and corresponded with their steward on the family's country estate.

"Almost." Her mother flicked through the sheets in her hands, counting silently. "I must finish Friday next and we shall have our meals arranged for a whole fortnight."

Penelope smiled, resuming her silence, and throwing her legs over the arm of her chair so she might recline in it. Watching her mother's sharp gaze traverse the pages before her, the quick movements of her quill, and the firm nod of her head, impressed on Penelope not for the first time the capability of her mother.

Just as Mrs Hughes returned with the tea tray, Lady Harwood shuffled the papers for the last time, and then handed them to the housekeeper.

"There you are, Mrs Hughes. It should make the food and drink purchasing as cost effective and as easy as possible."

"Very good, your Ladyship," said the servant, taking the menus and retreating from the room. As she passed Penelope she whispered, "Make sure Lady Harwood eats at least two of those pastries."

Penelope grinned at the housekeeper, winking conspiratorially.

"Would you pour, dear?" Lady Harwood asked, turning back to her desk and tidying away the writing implements into drawers and pots.

Her mother was terrible at looking after herself. No doubt Mrs Hughes' command was born of her Ladyship having forgotten to eat breakfast. Penelope supposed her father had been the one to notice and admonish his wife when he'd been alive.

"Here, Mama," said Penelope, holding a cup of steaming tea out to her mother.

"Thank you, my dear—dash it!" exclaimed Lady Harwood on seeing the state of her ink-stained fingers when she reached out for the welcome drink.

"Never mind that now," Penelope said, her arm beginning to ache. "Have your tea."

Her mother looked ready to argue, but the scent of hot tea was seemingly too tempting and she took the drink. After being coaxed into polishing off one pastry and taking another in hand, Lady Harwood looked much revived from a morning of taxing housekeeping.

"That Lord Standon has a liking for you, Penelope."

Her mother never did mince her words.

"Mama!" Penelope cried, almost spilling her tea and dreading instantly that her mother somehow knew about the kiss on the lakeside.

"Evidently your rudeness did not put him off." There was no response required. Her mother was so decided in her opinions and deductions. "Perhaps he has never had an eligible young miss do anything but trip over herself to compliment him."

Penelope caught a gleam in her mother's eye and the flash

of teeth soon hidden by the tea cup she sipped from. Her mother smiled so infrequently since her father died.

"I hardly think he does like me, Mama. His saving me on the lake was what any gentleman would do."

"I'm not sure Lord Fairing would have done the same," Lady Harwood replied frankly. "Far too undignified for a gentleman with such a high opinion of himself."

Penelope giggled. She had thought she was the only one who found Lord Fairing intolerably pompous.

"But do not let your sister hear me say so. She is positively smitten with his Lordship. I have no doubt we shall hear wedding bells by the Season's end."

"Good gracious, I hope not!" Penelope exclaimed, sitting up abruptly and clanking her tea cup down on the tray. "I don't know what she sees in him. The most odious dullard. Do you know he spent a full half-hour the other day explaining to me the finer points of polite behaviour that he likes to see in Society? It should have been polite of him to stop such fusty old prattle. The man has no feeling."

"A damning indictment indeed, my darling, but we all look for something different in our husbands." Her mother nibbled the last of her pastry. "I think perhaps your sister likes the propriety of Lord Fairing and the security it brings after your father's difficulties."

"I'm surprised he isn't bothered by them as others are," Penelope replied peevishly.

"While I expect the temptation is strong for you to apprise him of the ill-fortune of a connection with our family —to save yourself the acquisition of a brother—I would ask you not to for your sister's sake. I believe he genuinely holds affection for Thalia and that, along with the handsome fortunes your father has settled on both you girls, makes her quite palatable for his Lordship."

"I don't know why Thalia should care so for others' opinions. They will think the worst of us no matter what."

"Careful, Penelope. You sound bitter."

The rebuke smarted. Penelope shifted in her seat and pressed her lips together, pushing the thought of Lord Standon and his abrupt departure from her mind.

She wasn't bitter.

"What about Lord and Lady Etheridge at Sir Tristan's house party? I was there when you talked about them cutting you."

Was she bitter?

"Yes, but that's different. I wished to call a spade a spade. I held no desire to multiply false politeness and pretend nothing had occurred. To me that is as bad as lying. There is not allowing peoples' opinions and actions to define or affect you, and then there is being hostile towards others. I should never wish to hear you respond in such a manner, my child, for that is the way to bitterness. To be entirely frank, it takes far too much energy that is better spent on other things."

This was not at all how Penelope had envisaged this conversation going. She had come in here to ask her mother a question, and now she was reflecting on whether Lord Standon really had regretted kissing a Harwood woman.

"I only wish you to expend your efforts and energy on things worthy of them, my dear."

Her mother's words unknowingly pushed Penelope back on track.

"It is quite hard to ignore others' opinions when they believe our family to be—to be in possession of some great Stuart treasure."

Lady Harwood's expression changed instantly. The open, gentle look was sealed over with hardness.

"I thought that rumour had died with your father."

"So did I."

Her mother wasn't denying it.

"Is it—" Penelope halted, nervous. She knew her mother did not like talking about the details of the scandals surrounding her father. But if she did not ask now, she didn't know when else an opportunity would present itself. With Lady Spencer's words the other day and Lord Standon's warnings, Penelope needed to know the truth. "Is it true?"

Her mother replaced her empty cup in the saucer too quickly, the clatter making Penelope jump. She did not answer.

"I think it is my right to know if I am to carry these rumours throughout my life."

Her mother's gaze drifted over to the mantelpiece. Upon it sat a table clock in ebony and brass. It had been a gift from Lord Harwood to her mother. Penelope remembered listening to the music that would play when the clock struck the hour. Occasionally she'd catch her mother standing with a hand on the clock as the music played, tears in her eyes at the memory of the one who gave it to her.

The grief of her mother stirred up Penelope's own. A deep ache started in her chest as memories of her loving father crowded in. It was easier to talk of him now her grief was no longer fresh, but Penelope had been foolish not to realise how close to the surface it still was.

Could it be true that her father had been a Catholic and Jacobite sympathiser, and because of those beliefs which had caused so much damage, he had also been reckless enough to hide some priceless treasure for the exiled king?

Surely not. When Penelope had heard that rumour before, she had dismissed it as a fanciful tale borne from Society's penchant for scandal. Why not make the converted Catholic Lord Harwood the focus of the Government's Jacobite fears? If a man could change his faith at such an advanced age, there was no telling what else he was capable of. Harbouring such a treasure for the Old Pretender, perhaps?

"Do you suppose your father would have been unwise enough to harbour such a treasure, or I for that matter? What do you think that would mean for our family?" Her mother's gaze finally fell from the clock onto her daughter's face and Penelope immediately felt guilt at the expression of pain she saw.

Her suspicions were checked. Perhaps it was as fanciful as her mother had always portrayed. And yet, the rumour had been reignited in Society. According to Lady Spencer it was Count Feccio who had said it, and he had come from the Old Pretender's court in Italy. Where else could he have learned the story?

A horrid feeling slithered around Penelope's stomach. Were all the Harwood women as ignorant as each other? It *could* be true. And if it was true, what happened if he went further than threatening Lady Spencer and turned his attention to them?

Penelope realised that her mother was waiting for a response. She opted to answer the second question.

"It would not bode well for us."

"No," said Lady Harwood. "It would not. And I hope you think better of me than to allow such a risk to yours or Thalia's life."

Her Ladyship rose, placing her empty tea cup back on the tray.

"So, if anyone is as uncouth enough as to mention such a damaging rumour, you may tell them they are dull-witted!"

Lady Harwood's face shuttered over the grief that had been exposed. Her mother smoothed her skirts and checked her hair, signalling their conversation was at an end. They rarely spoke in such depth about her father and these painful rumours.

When Penelope and Thalia had come out in Society, their mother had sat them down and explained without detail the scandals that hung over their family. She had wished to prepare them, and she had done so with clear instructions not to entertain such vile tales. Apart from that, they spoke little about the rumours. Penelope knew this conversation had cost her mother dearly.

She withdrew her blue-eyed gaze from where it had drifted off to the middle distance and refocused on her mother who was straightening papers again on the desk. How she admired her parent's strength.

Jumping up suddenly from her chair, Penelope skipped over and embraced her.

"I love you, Mama," she whispered against her parent's shoulder, clinging to her like a child in short-coats.

"I love you too, my dear," said Lady Harwood, hugging her daughter back warmly.

The embrace lasted a minute longer, and then her mother released her, the moment over. Penelope saw Lady Harwood touch her fingers below each eye to capture any wayward tears before they fell down her cheeks and smudged her powder.

"Now I must be getting on. Your sister wishes to visit the milliner's shop when she's back, and I have letters to write before we may go. Off with you."

"Yes, Mama." Penelope nodded obediently, ringing the bell for the tea things to be cleared away before leaving her mother to her correspondence.

She had much to think on, never mind any silly kiss! She must determine what threat Count Feccio posed and prepare for Lady Spencer, who was due to call this afternoon when Mama and Thalia were out of the house.

CHAPTER 10

Penelope peered out of the morning room window for the fifth time.

Lady Spencer had been due to arrive a quarter of an hour ago, and ever since the conversation with her mother, the same words kept rolling around Penelope's mind.

If anyone is as uncouth enough as to mention such a damaging rumour...

The certainty that she was doing the right thing—aiding a woman in need—had fractured. Seeping through those cracks was the uncomfortable feeling of doubt. And then there were Lord Standon's warnings.

The bell sounded in the hall and a few moments later Lady Spencer swept into the room.

"Good morning, my child," she said, gliding forwards to take Penelope's hands in her own and squeeze them tightly to her chest. "What a balm it is to see you when I am being driven half-mad by nerves."

Nothing in the widow's faultless dress, collected state and unemotional gaze suggested such a truth.

"I am sorry to hear it," replied Penelope, guiding Lady

Spencer to the sofas and chairs scattered prettily around a low table. "If it is a consolation to you—you do not show it."

"I am fortunate then," replied her Ladyship, releasing Penelope and sweeping a hand across her figure. The immaculate state was topped off with a look of forlornness as though it all took great effort to achieve.

"Won't you sit?" Penelope asked.

The widow acquiesced, disappearing momentarily in a sea of pink silk and fur trimmings.

"I have gathered up all my pin money." Penelope pointed to the bulging coin purse sat in the middle of the low table. "Has the Count threatened you any further?"

"Oh, my dear—you are the best of girls."

Not women. *Girl.*

"He continues his onslaught."

"I was worried when I saw him in the same boat as you at Sir Tristan's house party. I did try to coax you into one with my sister and me." Penelope was trying her best to keep the suspicion from her voice.

"I know, my dear, I know." Lady Spencer sighed, spreading her arms in a gesture of graceful exasperation. "But he is so insistent and charming at times."

Charming? Penelope frowned.

Lady Spencer caught the look. "But his charm only conceals his ill intentions. And when I think of them I—" Her Ladyship's lips trembled.

She really did look like she was dwelling on some dreadful potentiality and Penelope immediately felt cruel for doubting her. "Will you take some tea, Lady Spencer? It may refresh you."

"Yes," Her Ladyship said absently, her eyes still on some far-off horror across the room. "Yes, I think I will." She fell back against the chair and lapsed into silence.

Penelope, thinking her guest's initial serenity had indeed

been masking an inner turmoil, sprang up from the sofa and rang the bell.

"I am sure a good cup of tea shall restore you. I shall order up some sweetmeats too."

In spite of the promise of tea, the colour appeared to leech from Lady Spencer's face. The woman did not respond. Was she going to swoon?

When Mrs Hughes appeared, Penelope ordered tea to be made with haste. After the housekeeper had retreated, Penelope came back to Lady Spencer, blue eyes wide with concern.

"I feel quite faint, my child." Her Ladyship lifted a weak hand to waft pathetically at her face. "Quite faint." Her breath was shallow and quick. "I need—I need hartshorn, my child, if you have it. Nothing else will revive me when I feel like this."

"Of course." Penelope should have suggested it herself. "I shall fetch Mama's."

Standing so rapidly she sent her chair rocking back on two legs, Penelope dashed from the room, leaving her patient now almost prostrate in her chair.

Racing across the hall and up the stairs, she headed for her mother's bedroom. Lady Harwood always kept her case of salts and restoratives somewhere in the room. Light poured into the homely chamber, illuminating the pretty feminine furniture and pale blue papers. Penelope ignored it all and headed straight to the nearest bedside table.

On it was a small portrait of her father, a Bible and a half-burned candle. The table and surrounding floor were clear of the familiar medicine box. She checked the other side, but it was the same. Perhaps her mother's grief had finally evolved past a need for daily restoratives.

Crossing over to the dressing table, she saw the old open gown her mother wore as a bedchamber covering hung over the back of the chair. Its old-fashioned skirts flared out across the floor. Penelope scanned the table top with its jars, pots and brushes. Another portrait of her father sat amongst them. It was from when her mother had first met him, showing him as a younger man dressed in a wide-skirted puce suit and heavy periwig. Penelope and Thalia often joked about it.

Penelope's gaze took all of this in quickly. Still no sign of the sought-after box. She turned back to the room, hands on hips, but still she could not spot the whereabouts of the desired object.

Where on earth was it?

She had never known her mother's bedroom without it. Thinking perhaps it was down in the kitchen to have its bottles refilled, Penelope gave a last sweeping glance of the room, before heading downstairs. That was when she caught sight of it.

"At last!" she exclaimed aloud, rushing back over to the dressing table and pulling the chair and her mother's robe away. Below the table, hidden by the skirts of the robe, was the box.

Pulling it out, thankful the key was still in the lock, Penelope slipped open the drop-front lid and scanned the array of bottles standing proud inside.

Recognising the hartshorn, she snatched it out triumphantly. Leaving the box as it was, she rushed back downstairs to Lady Spencer.

On gaining the hall, she saw the door of the morning room open. She entered to see Mrs Hughes setting the tea tray down next to the coin purse on the table.

"Oh, Lady Penelope!" Mrs Hughes jumped at her mistress' sudden appearance and threw a hand over her heart. "You gave me such a fright! I was just wondering where you and your guest had got to."

The chair in which Lady Spencer had laid prostrate moments ago was empty.

"Lady Spencer is not with me—she was not well." Penelope frowned. "Has she left?"

"Left?" Mrs Hughes' expression turned to one of bewilderment. "I don't think so, my Lady. I thought her still here visiting you. The front door has not gone and the footman's at his tea."

"I went to get Mama's smelling salts—she was here when I left her."

Penelope eyed the coin purse on the table. Surely Lady Spencer would not go without that.

"Her parasol and gloves are still in the hall," said Mrs Hughes, peering out of the morning room door.

The horrid feeling of doubt began to seep back through the cracks of Penelope's resolve.

Turning from the room, she re-entered the hall with Mrs Hughes and looked with fresh eyes.

The dining room door was open, but upon checking, Penelope found only one of the maids polishing the sideboard. The music room door was closed. She looked over to the final room—her mother's study. Her stomach dropped. It was ajar.

Pushing silently on the door, it swung back to reveal Lady Spencer by the mantelpiece, hand upon her father's clock, examining the case closely.

"Lady Spencer," Penelope said loudly.

"Oh! You startled me," scolded the widow.

"I have found Mama's hartshorn—though perhaps you no longer need it?" Penelope said archly, one brow rising. She was not in the least impressed by Lady Spencer's lack of bashfulness at being found so obviously snooping.

Lady Spencer smiled, completely unaffected by the tone, and dropped her hand from the clock as she turned to shrug at her young host. "You have caught me. A walk often aids me when I have an attack of the vapours. I could not resist having a wander through your beautiful home. I found myself here by accident." She gestured to her surroundings. "And I was quite taken by this beautiful clock."

By this time, Mrs Hughes had caught up with Penelope and was standing at her elbow like a kind of moral support. Penelope hated to admit she needed it.

"My, how severe you both look. I'm sorry to have given you a fright, but isn't it good I am recovered? Would you rather I still be close to fainting in the morning room?" Her manipulative words were like poison, sharp and wicked. "It is no matter." She wafted them away with her hand. "You have seen little of sickness in your time, my child, but sometimes one recovers quite miraculously."

Penelope had been able to swallow Lady Spencer's condescending tone when the widow had been in need of aid. Wandering unattended through her mother's study was quite another matter. Its coupling with this entitled attitude kindled Penelope's irritation into a fiery anger.

"But I feel I must return home and rest—you understand."

The high-handed conclusion was delivered so swiftly, Penelope wasn't given an opportunity to fully address the woman's strange behaviour. Her Ladyship immediately glided across the room and out into the hall. Her purposeful stride caused Penelope and Mrs Hughes to lurch out of the way. Had they not moved, Penelope was fairly certain Lady Spencer would have mowed them down.

"You must forgive me." Her Ladyship commanded as she picked up her parasol and gloves before heading for the front door. "I knew someone who had a clock like that. It makes me quite nostalgic."

The waiting footman—returned from his tea break— opened the front door of the Town house to make way for the imperious woman.

"He lives over the water now. I shall visit again." It wasn't a request and, touching a hand to her hat to check it was in place, she disappeared over the threshold.

"A gilflurt if ever I sees one," Mrs Hughes said under her breath.

Penelope was fairly sure she was not supposed to have heard those low words from the housekeeper, but she could not have agreed more. Lady Spencer was acting capriciously indeed.

Returning to the morning room alone, Penelope saw her coin purse was still sitting on the table, along with the undrunk tea.

What on earth had just happened? And why had Lady Spencer been examining that clock?

CHAPTER 11

Abandoning the tea things, Penelope went back to her mother's study and closed the door. She rested against it for a moment, staring at the clock from across the room.

Her father had taken great care over that clock. He had appeared as much attached to it as Penelope's mother, for whom it was a gift. Every week he would polish the oblong casing himself, cleaning the little brass feet and finials until they shone.

Penelope would go to the drawing room where it had pride of place and sit waiting for the musical chimes to sound as the clock struck the quarter hour. They didn't always sound, so it was like some playful game to see if they would each time, and she would run with glee to tell her papa when they did.

A lump formed in Penelope's throat at the memory—misty with time—playing across her mind. It brought with it the feeling of closeness they'd shared in those precious times.

"Why does it not play music every time, Papa?" she had asked once.

Her father had laid down his quill and smiled at her, not

vexed by the interruption. "It's a secret of the clock, my dear," he'd replied.

Teasing her—that's what she thought he had been doing. Elaborating on some mystery where there was none. It was the design of the clock.... wasn't it?

I knew someone who had a clock like that... he lives over the water now...

Lady Spencer's words pierced the happy memories and through those holes peered a question into Penelope's mind.

Over the water. She was not so naive that she did not recognise the euphemism for the Old Pretender.

Pushing off from the door, she strode purposefully over to the mantelpiece. Gazing up at the engraved brass face with its hands, she listened to the steady tick emanating from the clock. Her eyes slipped from the face to the body of the case, over the brass embellishments.

What had Lady Spencer been looking at?

With her face inches from the timepiece, all of a sudden it began to chime the quarter hour. Penelope squealed in surprise, jerking back. Shaking herself and giggling a little crazily in shock, she attempted to calm down before rolling forward onto her tiptoes again. Craning her neck, she tried to see round the back of the clock. Her eyes immediately took in a small drawer, slightly pulled out from its home, at the clock's base.

Lady Spencer hadn't just been *looking* at the clock.

Reaching up, Penelope took hold of the brass handles on either side of the timepiece and hefted the weighty object off the mantel. It landed with a soft thump on her mother's desk and took some manoeuvring to spin around so Penelope could access the back.

Above the little drawer, was a small glass window through which one could see the carefully crafted mechanism of the clock ticking ever forward. Gaze moving down, she took hold of the draw—designed with no handle to be flush with the clock's body and unnoticeable when closed—and eased it open.

Inside it was divided into three compartments. The two outer spaces were taken up by music barrels, their metal cylinders covered in little spokes that played those well-known tunes from Penelope's childhood. The central compartment, where presumably a third barrel *should* exist, held no such item.

A velvet pouch was pressed into the drawer.

Penelope's heart skipped a beat. That was why the clock did not always play a tune on the quarter hour. Her father's cryptic words had not just been some jest of a playful parent.

She reached into the compartment, pinched the pouch between her forefinger and thumb, and drew it out. It felt bulbous—there was something round inside. Turning it over in her hand she saw a leather flap and a metal clasp. She withdrew the hook of the clasp, flipped open the flap and turned the pouch upside down. Out into her palm dropped the clearest, most brilliant diamond she had ever seen.

Her jaw dropped. She gasped.

It was so large that she thought for a moment it must be glass. Surely it could not really be... but glass did not glitter like that.

She placed the empty velvet bag on the table and lay the gem atop it. Fear, sharp and potent, raged over her rational thoughts as she considered the possibility that the rumours which had dogged her family for years were true.

The reality stared her in the face with all its glittering facets. A king's ransom hidden away in a clock that had—according to Lady Spencer's implication—once belong to the Old Pretender. A fortune that could return an exiled king to a lost throne by financing an army.

Those great political considerations were lost to the ache

of Penelope's heart. She could accept never understanding her father's beliefs, but the idea they had overridden his duty as a husband and father to protect his family was... devastating.

She could hardly believe it of him. Clearly her mother did not. After this morning's conversation there was no way Lady Harwood could know about the diamond in the clock. Penelope's father had trusted in her mother's sentimentality. Lady Harwood would never give away or sell an object gifted in affection, especially after his death.

How could he have done such a thing?

For so many years it had lain hidden and harmless in that musical clock—until Lady Spencer had arrived. There was only one way the widow could have known where to look for the gem. She had to be working on behalf of the exiled king. Travelling from Italy. Befriending Penelope. Playing on Penelope's feelings concerning her father. It had all been to gain access to the Harwood residence and retrieve the diamond.

No one could find out about this.

Picking up the diamond and dropping it back in the pouch, Penelope replaced the treasure in the drawer of the clock and shut it away. It had remained hidden there for twenty-three years, and if it wasn't for Lady Spencer, Penelope might have chosen to forget all about it again.

Lifting the clock onto the mantelpiece, she carefully manoeuvred it back to where it had always sat, to arouse no suspicions from her mother. Beginning a vigorous pacing of the room, she began to think. She could still feel the weight of that diamond in her hands, heavy enough to drag all her family down.

Who else knew about the diamond?

How far would the treacherous Lady Spencer go to get it?

And most importantly, what on earth should she do now?

CHAPTER 12

"The Fairings'?" Roderick's father questioned his son's destination that evening while the two of them sipped port after dinner. "You realise their son has some kind of connection with the younger Harwood girl? I should think the whole family will be in attendance."

Yes, Roderick realised that. In fact, he was counting on their connection to necessitate their attendance tonight, so that he might bump into Lady Penelope. He hadn't seen her since Sir Tristan and Lady Belvedore's house party. Since... that kiss...

"Still, a far safer excursion than a lake where those wild girls are concerned," his father blustered.

Where Lady Penelope was concerned, Roderick did not share his father's confidence. Safety was never guaranteed. And indeed, it was the subject of her safety for which Roderick wished to see her. The enquiries he had left Sir Tristan's house party to pursue in London—regarding the widow Lady Spencer and her hanger-on Count Feccio—had been most enlightening.

"For the sake of my clothes this evening, I do hope there

will be no water features," Roderick replied, a crease appearing at the corner of his mouth.

"Well, if it pleases you to go, then go, my boy," replied his father gruffly. "But take my advice and avoid those Harwood women. It isn't just lakes that make them dangerous."

No, Roderick thought. It was their kisses too.

Ever since he had felt the soft warmth of Lady Penelope Harwood's lips, he had found his mind consumed with the idea of feeling them again.

"Their father casts a long shadow."

"Are we still in the habit of blaming the sins of the father upon the child?"

"Who says they are not the sins of the children too?" asked his father, his belligerent tone not abating. "Who's to say what those Harwood women think? For all we know they could have converted to Catholicism themselves! Not to mention their wilfulness. Lady Harwood is as headstrong as she's always been—it's why I warned your mother off her when Lord Harwood converted to Catholicism and started his ill-conceived connections with the Stuart court. Showed no remorse for her husband's dealings. She might not be known for supporting the Jacobite cause, but her lack of censure for her husband's affiliations is contemptible."

Roderick frowned. Deriding a wife for loyalty to her spouse hardly seemed fair.

"The taint that such behaviour causes affects the blood. And they may have held onto their place in polite Society by the skin of their teeth, but that does not mean they deserve it, nor that we should humour them. It was badly done of Sir Tristan to invite them to his house party without first warning us. I have not been forced to greet Lady Harwood since her foolish husband's demise. It quite upset your mother. She has not stopped talking about how poor Athena must have struggled since Lord Harwood's death, and I've had a dashed awful time of it trying to keep her from visiting the woman." His father had successfully worked himself up into a fret now and was pounding his fist on the arm of his chair.

There was little point in highlighting the high-handedness of his father's opinions, nor the commendable compassion his mother wished to show Lady Harwood. Just as Lady Penelope's mother was a fierce woman protecting her family, so was Roderick's father in protecting his from what he perceived as a threat.

Roderick deemed it even more prudent than before, that he not speak of his dealings with Lady Penelope. Not wishing to leave his father in a pucker, Roderick turned the subject to the latest race at Newmarket. It did the trick, and they spent the next quarter of an hour debating who were the most desirable sires and dams in the racing world at present. Leaving his father somewhat mollified, he tossed off the rest of his port and took his leave.

Off to the Fairings' he went, with a clear mission in mind.

The atmosphere in the Fairings' rather ostentatious salon, decorated after the French style, was raucous. Roderick entered to a cacophony of voices. People laughed, conversed, jested, and exclaimed all at once. The whole room was being heavily lubricated by wine which servants poured plentifully into out-held glasses, and the glow from a hundred candles blazed from sparkling chandeliers.

A musician took the edge off the loudness of the company. He was playing a harpsichord in the corner and Roderick recognised one of Bach's recent compositions. Navigating the card tables and the crowds gathered to observe them, he made his way through the throng.

To his left a table erupted in cheers at an apparent win and another wave of heat from the crowds and candles assailed him. Who knew the dull dog Fairing had a family who could lay on such festivities?

Several individuals greeted him as he passed, adjuring him to join their tables for the next hand. He glimpsed a more sedate game of what looked like quadrille over the other side of the room—farthest from the music—and spied Fairing and the young Lady Thalia playing.

Excellent. That meant his gamble had been worth it. If the younger Harwood sister were in attendance, the elder was more than likely here as well.

"Standon, old boy." Sir George hailed him.

His peer had been engaged in watching a game of cards on a nearby table, but broke away to greet his friend.

"Good to see you, Sir George."

"Well met." The smiley gentleman grasped Roderick's arm warmly. "I had it from Mires you were back from the country. Sir Tristan's wasn't it?"

"That's right." Roderick continued to look around the room for his quarry. "A nice break from the city."

"Shame about his connection to trade—poor man can't help it, but it does leave a pall over his gatherings, don't you think?"

He'd forgotten this about his friend. Despite only being a baronet, Sir George was a stickler for rank. Many of Roderick's friends called him a knight and barrow pig for his pretensions to precedency, not that he would join in such vulgar talk.

"I hadn't noticed." Or cared. "The man's business acumen is hard to rival. I found it directly translated to the running of my family's estate when discussing it with him. He's given me ideas for several improvements to discuss with my father."

Sir Tristan was a good man, friendly to a fault. Roderick had wondered how such a magnanimous individual could manage such a profitable business in turnpike trusts and road building. Yet a visit to his newly built country house could leave no one in doubt as to the man's commercial success.

"Oh, of course, the man has brain—I'll give him that. And he's amiable enough. Certainly helped himself with his choice of wife. Excellent blood. No doubt his in-laws' imminent bankruptcy helped his suit. But one can always sense connections with trade."

"You think so?" Roderick would not be drawn into such unnecessary denigration.

Everyone knew Sir Tristan's marriage was one of convenience and yet it had blossomed into a love match. The repetition of such information only seemed to confirm Sir George's lack of character.

"Perhaps we should take Voltaire's view from his *Letters to the English*," said Roderick. "It is those in trade who 'contribute to the felicity of the world', not us men of birth. You may choose not to associate with Sir Tristan, but I shall not be accused of turning down felicity." Roderick chuckled. "Nor the acquaintance of a good man. You'd do well to throw your notions of snobbery away where Sir Tristan is concerned."

"Far be it from me to scorn felicity," Sir George blustered, colour staining his cheeks as he took in the pointed words of his friend. "You always were one to take no notice of reputation, Standon."

"You do me a wrong there," Roderick replied, "I simply do not accept another person's opinions on an individual. I form my own—without any bias from other sources. It may agree with the reputation I have previously heard about, but more often than not, I find others' opinions can be a little—ah —one-sided, for my taste."

Sir George began to bluster in response, his tone oscillating between peeved and surprised at his friend's rebuff.

"Now, forgive me," Lord Standon said, interrupting the

man's fretting, "but I must excuse myself in favour of a lady's company."

He had spied Lady Penelope off to the left, standing in a window embrasure with her back to the room.

"But of course, I only meant that..." Sir George struggled to justify himself, but his words were lost to the crowd through which Roderick made his way.

Turning off a second attempt to waylay him, Roderick at last reached Lady Penelope, coming to stand at her elbow.

His approach went unnoticed as her back was to the room. Even now, with him at her side, she stared unblinking out of the window. Her attention was miles away and to Roderick's surprise, he saw she had removed one of her gloves and was chewing distractedly on her thumbnail.

"I thought for a moment that I might have found you talking to a window this time, instead of a painting."

Lady Penelope jolted, blue eyes snapping up to Roderick's face. She said nothing. He waited for a set down, a barbed comment, a scold, but she just stared at him before turning back to the window and resuming her study of the world beyond the glass.

Strange. Or rather, stranger than usual.

He tried again. "Or have you come away from the crowds to this secluded place to think? What about, I wonder?"

He attracted Lady Penelope's gaze, but he did not like the look in her eyes.

"Good evening, Lord Standon." Her delayed greeting was delivered in an icy tone.

The kiss!

How could he have forgotten? He hadn't entirely, but in truth he'd been distracted by searching out the truth regarding Lady Spencer. What he'd found out had consumed his thoughts when considering meeting Lady Penelope again.

She must think him a scoundrel.

"You do not appear to be having a good evening, Lady Penelope. I must apologise for my behaviour when last we met —" He broke off. This was a great deal harder than he'd thought it would be. "I have not acted like a gentleman. No doubt this is why you, quite understandably, greet me with such coldness?"

"Coldness?" she asked, bewildered, dropping her hand from her mouth. "I regret to inform you, my Lord, that you do not feature in my thoughts at all."

The frankness was entirely her, yet her words smarted. He had thought of little else but Lady Penelope since they'd met.

"I am all relief, my Lady. May I then trespass on your goodwill to discuss with you something I have recently been made aware of?"

"I am a little busy," she replied without pause.

This second rebuff was enough to destroy even the most robust man's confidence. If it wasn't for the need to speak to Lady Penelope on a subject important to her welfare, he might have given up for the night.

"Busy?"

"I'm thinking." She nodded, gaze firmly on the stars appearing above the roofline opposite.

"I promise I shall not intrude on your thinking longer than strictly necessary."

"Oh, very well, my Lord." She tossed her hands up in the air in exasperation and swivelled to face him. "What is it you wish to say?"

"I realise I have tried your patience several times on this subject, but I must again turn to the person of Lady Spencer." He raised his hand pre-emptively to stop any outburst that might be coming. To his surprise though, none of her previous indignation showed on her face. "I have heard—"

"What has she said?"

Roderick noted the sudden hint of panic in her voice, the wideness of her eyes.

"She?" he queried. "You mistake me. I have not spoken to Lady Spencer. Rather, I have heard a tale to the contrary of the one she told you about the gentleman, Count Feccio."

He expected a rebuttal at that assertion, but none came.

"I believe you thought her Ladyship in danger from that gentleman. However, I now have it on good authority that she has led you astray with such implications. I've discovered that she did, in fact, arrive on our shores in the Count's company. I should not wish to shock you, so I will not call it what it is, but I am sure you can surmise the nature of their real relationship.

"I have also found out, upon making enquiries, that they have both been visiting prominent families known to sympathise with the Stuart cause. So, you see, my concerns over your friendship with the lady are well-founded. Though, I hasten to add, I take no pleasure in confirming my suspicion to you. Of more concern, though, is why she would use such a falsehood to befriend you."

"I have a fair idea."

She muttered the words, so Roderick wasn't sure she meant for him to hear.

"You suspected?"

Her gaze darted up to his face. Her eyes held the look of someone who wished they hadn't uttered their thoughts aloud. This was not how he had expected this conversation to play out.

"No."

More puzzling still.

"I have been a complete fool," she said sourly. "And you have only been trying to help me all this time. What prompted you to make enquiries?"

"Concern for your welfare, Lady Penelope," he replied honestly.

She stilled. The fretting of her hands twisting the glove she held, the tapping of her right foot on the ground, the darting of her eyes—it all stopped. Her blue gaze locked onto his.

"I have been worried for you." He reached up, touching his hand to the top of her arm, rubbing his thumb over her sleeve. "I only hope this deception has not hurt your feelings too deeply."

"My feelings? Those are of little consequence."

"Not to me."

"What you must think of me—what Society must think of my family," she exclaimed.

"Society can be foolish sometimes. It is best not to pay it much heed."

A wan smile appeared on her face. "You sound like my mother."

"I shall take that as a compliment," he replied ruefully.

"Please do. Oh, how I have let her down! How I have let poor Thalia down!"

Roderick was horrified to see tears in Lady Penelope's lovely eyes.

"My Lady—Penelope." He had stopped stroking her arm, but now took up the hand closest to him. "You are too harsh on yourself."

"You do n-not understand," she stammered, the tears now falling down her smooth cheeks.

"Please, tell me what is the matter? Let me help you."

"Forgive me, Lord Standon. I am not myself this evening. I-I must retire." She pulled her hands from his grip and hurried away through the crowds before he could stop her.

He tried to find her again later, but heard from his host that the Harwoods had retired early due to Lady Penelope taking ill. They'd been sad to see her go, and poor Lady Thalia had complained most bitterly about it.

Roderick left shortly after, nothing keeping him at the Fairings now that Lady Penelope had gone. What was it that he could not understand? What on earth had Lady Spencer done?

CHAPTER 13

It was quite simple. Penelope would cut Lady Spencer from her acquaintance. That would do the trick. No more tête-à-têtes, no more proclamations of friendship, no more offers of aid. She must protect her family, just as her mother had done.

Several days had passed and lifted the fog of uncertainty to reveal the structure of falsehood below. It was clear now that Lady Spencer must have known about the clock all along. She had played Penelope's feelings like a spinet, hitting notes she knew would elicit the responses she required, and gain from her access to Harwood House. The truly hurtful part was that her Ladyship had pretended to be battling the same dark cloud of rumours as the Harwood women.

Jacobite sympathiser. The widow had pretended to fight against the same injustice of being lumped together with her traitorous husband. The manipulative woman had done it all because she knew that poor, naive little Lady Penelope would behave like a puppet on a string if she told that tale.

How foolish Penelope had been!

Pish! There was no use dwelling on it now. She pushed

away the sick feeling in her stomach. That diamond must never see the light of day. She could not let her mother and sister know the threat they faced. Lady Spencer, to all intents and purposes, no longer existed.

That last resolution was what made it so very impertinent of the woman to appear in the flesh at an exhibition the Harwoods were attending. *Loathsome.* Penelope's only recourse was to cut her acquaintance at the first opportunity.

"Can't we summer in Margate?" Thalia was whining at their mother again and Lady Harwood was doing an excellent job of ignoring her. Her Ladyship appeared to be wafting her younger daughter's words away with her fan.

"How can I be expected to answer such quizzing," asked her Mama, finally giving in on the third repetition of the question, "when we have only faced half the Season?"

"Faced?" Thalia replied indignantly. "You say it like it's some great chore."

"Not all of us are blessed with your steadfast suitor, Thalia," Penelope said, eyes on her foe, Lady Spencer, who was examining statues across the hall.

"You have Lord Standon," Thalia countered.

"No, I do not!" Penelope glared at her sister. "Besides, what is this sudden obsession with that resort town? You've never mentioned it before."

"I think," said their mother, employing a far calmer tone than either of her daughters, "it is, perhaps, where a certain Lord Fairing and his family are intending on summering. Is that right, Thalia?"

"He has spoken of the benefits of the town."

"Transparency itself, my dear." Lady Harwood's lips curved into a knowing smile. "And I have to agree with Thalia, my dear Penelope. I saw Lord Standon seek you out most particularly at the Fairings' party. How was he?"

Her mother was always so abominably sharp.

"He was"—Penelope struggled to find a replacement for the truth—"checking on my health after the incident on the lake."

Her mother made no reply, slowly wafting her fan as she bestowed a piercing gaze upon her elder daughter. A second later she lifted one sceptical brow.

"Oh, stop it, Mama. Aren't we supposed to be looking at Italian statues?" Penelope swivelled to look at the nearest piece of sculpted marble. It focused on a vestal virgin with a veil draped over her face. The mournful figure looked so lifelike. Penelope felt she could reach out and draw the soft material from the woman's head.

"I'm surprised," her mother murmured in her ear, "that such an enquiry after your health would result in tears, my child."

She could not tell her mother the truth. That his Lordship's well-intentioned interference had prompted Penelope to realise her naivety. A naivety which had put her whole family in danger.

"The Fairings' candles were so smoky that night. I can hardly be blamed for being affected by them."

"Ah, the candles." Her mother's fine brow had not dropped.

"Shall we go on to the next statue? This one is so maudlin."

Thalia had a point.

The Harwood party moved on and Penelope was just focusing on a stone depiction of Persephone, when a figure rounded the plinth on which the Greek goddess perched.

"Ah, my friend, Penelope."

For the first time since meeting her, Penelope could hear the honied tones for what they were—false. And she noted Lady Spencer had dropped her title without permission.

The widow was dressed in a heavily embroidered yellow

casaquin and matching skirt. The linen bodice of the hip-length coat, with its wide back pleats and heavy sleeve folds, had a dipped front to show off a stunning set of pearls. The edge of the bodice and sleeves were trimmed with intricate pleating of the same botanically embroidered cloth, and her hat displayed matching dyed yellow feathers.

"I was *so* hoping to see you again. I must thank you for your kind offer of aid. I only realised after I had left your house that I had not taken it with me. So paper-skulled of me! I was quite turned about by my sudden faintness."

Penelope said nothing. She was hoping Lady Spencer would get the hint and leave.

"I shall call on you again," the widow continued, immune to Penelope's stony expression, averted gaze and silence. "When your sister and mother are out, of course, for I do not wish to attract attention. No doubt, your younger sister will be keen to call on Lord Fairing and his family soon."

The entitlement of her words grated like a knife on earthenware. Penelope followed the woman's overt look towards where Thalia was standing with her mother, talking to Lord Fairing. Her sister's cheeks coloured becomingly as she looked up at her suitor.

"Shall we say Thursday?"

The nerve of this woman!

"No."

Penelope had hoped only to have to ignore her, but apparently this woman wasn't taking the hint.

"Oh, my child." Lady Spencer wafted herself with a matching yellow fan. "You surprise me. Have I upset you?"

Penelope finally turned towards the widow. Lady Spencer had the same beautiful face, fine nose, full mouth and alluring eyes. Yet Penelope could now see something else. Something deeper. A truth beneath that mask of affected politeness. A truth she was not privy to.

How had she not seen that dissembling before?

"I see you are in the company of Count Feccio once again," Penelope said accusingly, one hand on her hip.

"Him?" Lady Spencer turned to where the gentleman waited some way off. Though the Count spoke to another man nearby, it was clear from his frequent glances towards her Ladyship, that he waited for her. "He insists. The pressure he puts me under. I can hardly bear it. That is why I hoped to visit you again soon. It mortifies me to ask for your aid, but you were so good as to offer it before, and you have no under-standing of how much it shall assist me."

"I can bring it to your home," said Penelope, a sudden idea darting into her mind.

"So kind, but I am happy to retrieve it. I should not wish to put you out. You have already done so much for me."

"It would be no bother," Penelope replied. "When shall I come? Thursday?"

"No, no." Lady Spencer reached out and pressed her hand against the one Penelope still rested on her hip.

The urge to swat the widow away was strong.

"I shall come to you again. I hope... I hope I did not offend you, my friend, by my little— ah—wander around Harwood house. It is only that it helps me when I feel—"

"Oh, please do stop it!" Penelope hissed under her breath.

She felt her own stupidity in this moment so keenly she couldn't carry on. It was all so dreadfully obvious now. Lady Spencer was after the diamond and Penelope had been too pig-headed to see her manoeuvring. She had been too busy thinking herself the heroine and basking in the glory of it all.

"Are you quite well, Penelope?" the widow asked, wafting herself with her fan and affecting a mildly caring expression. Was it too much to believe someone was denying her? Was she imagining the poor young Harwood girl must be ill?

"I may have been foolish enough to swallow your story whole, but I won't do so anymore," Penelope said. "The Count holds no sway over you except one of affection. Your story about requiring aid was a ruse—I knew it the moment I found you in my mother's study. And now you think I shall just let you in my home again? You are no more my friend than this statue here." She gestured angrily at Persephone's fossilised figure before them.

Her barked words hung in the air between them. Penelope's heart raced, and she half expected her false friend to run away in tears. She hoped she would—or did she? A twinge of guilt. No! She must remain strong.

Lady Spencer sighed. "How disappointing."

Penelope risked a glance at her foe. There was no harried expression, no sorrowful look, no deep shock. Lady Spencer fanned herself in the same unhurried way she had done before, and in fact, her expression took on a look of ennui.

"I had hoped to carry on the ruse a little longer and spare you from the alternative."

Alternative?

Icy dread crept into Penelope's stomach.

No! She wouldn't be led on a merry dance by this woman anymore. She couldn't believe a word she said.

"At least admit it. You stole your way into my confidence under false pretences just so you could get to—" Penelope broke off, glancing around them to make sure no one would overhear.

"So, you found it!" Lady Spencer's eyes gleamed. "My patron was very specific about where I might find his property when he dispatched me to recover it. You should be thanking me. I might have used more base methods, but I chose to spare your family that. Besides, it is in my interests as much as yours to retrieve it quietly.

"At least I attempted to. It *was* rather easy. Such an innocent you turned out to be, dear little Penelope. You couldn't wait for the chance to help a poor, harassed widow."

Penelope's apprehension grew. Lady Spencer's admission made it feel all too real, and she seemed unaffected by her exposure. Penelope had dipped her toe into these dangerous waters to confront the widow, but she was inadvertently being pulled out of her depth.

"If you wish only to insult me, I shall leave."

"Not so fast, little miss!" Lady Spencer reached out and grabbed her arm, fingers vice-like, holding her fast. "Let's walk together." She moved her grip onto Penelope's hand, pulling it through her arm and dragging her forward to walk around the exhibits. "Don't struggle, Lady Penelope. We wouldn't want to cause a scene. Especially as I have in my possession a letter from the rightful king to your father that would condemn your family name forever."

Penelope was arrested on the verge of yanking her arm free.

"What are you talking about?" she demanded, but Lady Spencer ignored her.

"Good girl," said the widow as Penelope began walking with her.

Gracious, how she wished to strike this woman.

"You must realise that up until now you have been a child, and I have treated you as such. But this is an adult game you have chosen to play, and there is far more at stake than your precious pride."

"You lying snake!" Penelope hissed under her breath, forcing a smile onto her face as they passed acquaintances. "There is no such letter."

"Name-calling is uncouth, my child," Lady Spencer said, patting Penelope's hand on her arm. "I thought you might suspect something after finding me in your mother's study. In case of that eventuality, I have brought the item with me to persuade you that our interests are aligned."

Cold fear coursed through Penelope's veins. Exchanges were happening all around them about inconsequential nothings—observations about the statues on display or who was here to be seen. All as if her family's fate did not hang in the balance.

Lady Spencer was as collected as Penelope was wild. It made it all worse. Such poison as she was spewing, with no inkling of shame or remorse, and no thought to the damage she was causing.

They came to the end of the exhibits and the widow had steered them into a little alcove. She released Penelope and reached into her reticule, extracting from it a letter. With her back to the room to shield what she was doing from public gaze, she held the letter out close enough so that Penelope might see the broken seal. A rose with Latin inscription cracked in two.

Penelope began to feel nauseous.

"Uh-uh." Lady Spencer snatched it away as Penelope reached for it.

"That could be any letter."

Lady Spencer smiled with all the confidence of one who already knew they'd won the game. She unfolded the letter and held it so that Penelope might read it,

My Lord Harwood,

I am well informed and very sensible of the services perform'd to the Crown by your ancestors, and now your own freely given loyalty. I am moved to let you know my resolution of creating you a Duke. I here promise that you shall be the first of the

Dukes of Harwood, and I will take your person, and your family, into my care to recompense your past and future services.

With every word Penelope took in, the cold dread she had been feeling grew, until it became an engulfing terror.

You shall become an argument to encourage others to serve me zealously, and I ask your services again here. I am delivering you of this clock, and the treasure that lies within, in the hopes that when I may return for it, you will deliver it into my hands, and I may be restored to my rightful throne under God with the aid it may provide.

There it was, in bold ink, her father's betrayal.

Our defeat at Preston has left me no choice but to return to the Continent, and now my fever abates, I shall sail on the first tide. What I now promise to you in this letter, and in turn beg from you in covenant of safekeeping, I do so by the concurrence and consent of the Queen, my dearest mother.

James R, Montrose, 2nd February, 1716

Penelope shook as Lady Spencer re-folded the letter and placed it back in her bag.

"Trust me, I have no interest in ruining some insignificant family's reputation."

Penelope gasped. "Trust you?"

"*But*," Lady Spencer continued, "if you force my hand... well... then you shall see just how dangerous I can be and this damning little letter will find its way into the public light. This is far bigger than you or I, and these pathetic parties and fanciful balls. This is about the future of our country and—"

"Spare me," Penelope snapped, shock wearing off and her temper returning. "I have no interest in the political games you play. Only in how they affect my family."

"That is the problem with all of you." Lady Spencer stepped back to gesture around the room. "No vision of what could be, what should be—just blind, foolish acceptance of what is. I am disgusted with what this country has become. I see a court following the whims of some foreign King who cares nothing for this land and its heritage. Who are the Hanovers when compared to the divine right of the Stuart house?" Lady Spencer asked.

Penelope wished to walk away. But in the embrace of that innocuous yellow reticule lay the means to ruin her family forever. She had to find a way to stop this woman.

"You say you have no interest in politics," Lady Spencer said, "and yet you have a part to play, my young friend. That clock—the one sitting on the mantelpiece of your family's study—it was a gift to your father. He was given it for safe-keeping, and I work for the one who bestowed it. I want you to give it to me in exchange for this letter." She patted her bag.

Penelope inhaled sharply.

"I know what you're thinking—would she really do such a wicked thing?" Lady Spencer smiled, like a cat circling an injured bird.

"I have no such doubts," Penelope replied. Her voice sounded weak and she could not bring herself to look into Lady Spencer's smug face.

"Good. Then you will give me the clock."

The sound of Thalia laughing came from across the room

and Penelope glanced over to see her younger sibling enjoying the company of Lord Fairing. So innocent while Penelope talked with someone so sordid.

What a fool she had been.

"You have until the end of tomorrow to bring it to me—and do not think to remove its contents." Lady Spencer sighed. "This is why I tried my hardest to trick you. Ignorance would have been so much better for you and I might have slipped off quietly, but now you've gone and ruined it all. You are innocent to a fault, my child, so determined to help. Perhaps I have done you a good turn exposing you to all this."

Penelope raged from one emotion to another. Humiliation at her own naivety and anger at Lady Spencer's arrogance.

"It's simple," the widow said in slow, over-enunciated words, as if to a child. "You don't deliver the clock, I release the letter. You deliver the clock, you save your family and whatever reputation your father has left—understand?"

Mind galloping through all the scenarios and finding no way out of this coil, all Penelope could do was glare at the heinous woman.

"I shall need more than a look, my child. *Do you* understand?"

"Yes," said Penelope quietly. "I understand."

"Good." She pressed her direction into Penelope's hand. "Now, you will excuse me. The Count is waiting."

With a flourish of her yellow skirts, Lady Spencer turned and glided away. Penelope toyed with the idea of running after her and snatching that reticule from her hands. As if that would help. The woman would likely scream the place down and everyone present would learn of the letter. Bringing attention to this horrible, impossible situation, would be the worst thing to do. She knew that.

The widow took up the Count's arm and whispered something in his ear. The couple fell to laughing. What fun it was to deceive a stupid young girl and threaten her family. The Count's hand was around Lady Spencer's waist as they walked away into the crowds. They could not be anything but lovers as Lord Standon had hinted. It had all been one colossal falsehood.

The fury Penelope had felt in the presence of the taunting lady was cooling quickly. In its place, the icy fingers of dread were threading their way around her mind and chest. If she didn't hand over the clock, her family would be enveloped in scandal. If she did, she would be complicit with Jacobite sympathisers, and there was no guarantee the dishonest widow would keep the Old Pretender's letter a secret. Surely the dastardly lady would release it regardless to throw suspicion away from herself and Count Feccio?

Whichever way Penelope looked at it, she and her family were doomed. Absolutely doomed.

CHAPTER 14

Roderick had observed the exchange between Lady Spencer and Lady Penelope from across the exhibition gallery. He had noticed their discreet positioning and despite his best efforts, he could not gain sight of Lady Penelope's face. But it was obvious from the mannerisms that were visible, she appeared agitated.

When Lady Spencer left her young friend, Roderick took his chance and made his way to Lady Penelope's side. The beautiful young woman broke her stare from an arrangement of flowers in a Grecian urn at the back of the alcove and glanced fleetingly at him. One arm was wrapped around herself, the other rested atop it, and her gloved fingers were tapping an unknown beat upon her lips. She inclined her head slightly in greeting.

"Good day, Lady Penelope. I could not help but observe your conversation with Lady Spencer from across the room. Is it safe to assume, from your agitation, that you have severed your acquaintance with the woman? I hope it was not too unpleasant for you."

"Would that I could have!" Lady Penelope burst out, her

state of aggravation far higher than he realised. She cast her hands suddenly in the air and almost sent the flowers she'd been gazing at crashing to the floor.

Roderick jerked a hand forward to steady the pediment.

"Lady Penelope, what is it? What has occurred?"

"That woman—oh—that woman!" Her blue eyes blazed, her face flush with indignant colour, her slender shoulders drawn back ready for battle. Despite his concern over her welfare, he had to admit that, in this moment, the small woman before him was formidable.

"She has said something to upset you? I urge you to pay it no heed," said Roderick, trying to comfort her. "She cannot force her acquaintance upon you if you do not wish it. My sister is forever cutting people for the silliest of causes. Yours is a substantial reason."

"It's not that, it's—" She began wringing her hands.

In an instant, the fierceness in her face dissolved. The wide eyes and clear brow crumpled all at once and she turned quickly to the wall to hide her emotions from him.

"My dear, Lady Penelope." Roderick did his best to move slowly, so as not to attract attention. It took considerable willpower to hold back from immediately embracing her.

"Here." He offered his handkerchief discreetly.

"N-no, I shall r-ruin it," she stammered between silent sobs.

"Will you please desist from being stubborn for five minutes and allow me to do you this service." He pressed the handkerchief into her hands and to his satisfaction, she took it, and smiled through tear-filled eyes up at him.

"Th-thank you," she said, dabbing at her face and sniffing until the sobs subsided. "I do so hate to cry. You must think me abominably goosish."

"Nonsense," he replied firmly. "Now please tell me how I may assist you."

"I cannot." She turned a little from the wall towards him.

"Ah! But you saying you cannot tell me, lets me know there is indeed something afoot in which I may intercede."

She stared down at the wilted handkerchief in her hands.

"Please." He stepped forward, shielding their interaction a little from the room, and took both her hands in his. "Allow me to help you."

"There is nothing you can do. Nothing even I can do but what she has asked—"

"Roderick!"

His mother's voice sounded behind him. Releasing Lady Penelope's hands, after pressing them gently, he turned to see his approaching relative. What ill-timing.

"Mother." He inclined his head, pausing to give his companion time to compose herself before stepping to the side and revealing her. "You remember, Lady Penelope Harwood."

"Lady Etheridge." The young woman curtseyed prettily and managed a courageous smile.

"Lady Penelope, I have just seen your mother and sister."

"I wasn't aware you and father were attending this exhibition," said Roderick, irritated by the interruption and painfully aware he had not discovered the truth of Lady Penelope's upset. What on earth had Lady Spencer demanded she do?

"Your father wished to see Lord Anthony and Sir Tristan and understood them to be in attendance here. He sent me over when he saw you."

His father had not wished to converse with a Harwood himself, that's what she meant.

"Are you enjoying the exhibition, my dear?" asked Lady Etheridge.

His mother was always kind, in spite of his father. Dressed as she was in an old-fashioned mantua gown, its train pinned back to display silver embroidery on green, a small cap on her coiffure with lace lappets draping over her shoulders, she not only sounded, but looked the mothering figure.

"Not terribly, your Ladyship," said Lady Penelope.

Such honesty was wholly in keeping with her character, and Roderick couldn't help his mouth curve upwards at her courage.

"I must apologise for looking so wretched." She pressed the handkerchief again to her cheeks. "Your son has been very kind to me."

"Oh, my dear, I'm sorry to see it. Perhaps we might find a quiet corner where you may take a moment to recover?"

Roderick resisted the urge to say they were already in a quiet corner.

"Roderick, your father wishes to speak to you. I can remain with Lady Penelope."

Ah, so that was it. His father had sent over his mother to extract their son from the clutches of a Harwood. Roderick glanced over to where his father stood and saw that, although his parent was conversing with Lord Anthony, he was surreptitiously looking over to the alcove.

"Of course," Lady Penelope said, her voice stronger than before.

Roderick saw her quick blue eyes flit between himself, his mother and his father over yonder. She had gathered the state of affairs quickly.

"I have taken up too much of your son's time already. Please, Lord Standon, feel released and here." She offered his handkerchief back to him.

He bowed. "Please keep it, Lady Penelope. Your need is greater than mine." He gently pushed the handkerchief back to her, rubbing a thumb over her hand as he did so.

His mother cleared her throat.

"Good day to you. I shall call on you soon." He shot a challenging look at his mother and then turned and left.

From the far side of the room, he watched his mother speak quietly to Lady Penelope, and gently walk her to another space devoid of people. While his female parent might be operating under the instructions of his father, he knew his mother to be compassionate, and was sure she was doing what she could to soothe Lady Penelope's frayed nerves.

Roderick paid little heed to his father and Lord Anthony's conversation. It was clear within minutes Lord Etheridge had no need of him and so he lapsed into silence.

Nothing even I can do, but what she has asked.

Those had been Lady Penelope's words.

He could not leave her alone to face whatever nastiness Lady Spencer had thrown at her. His heart simply wouldn't let him.

CHAPTER 15

"I hope very much it is not my son who has upset you," said Lady Etheridge, searching Penelope's face as they sat together on a bench at the far end of the gallery.

Without Lord Standon's penetrating hazel eyes, Penelope found it much easier to regain her composure. She had no wish to display her emotions before a woman she barely knew, and there was always something about Lord Standon that brought out the truth of Penelope's feelings. It was exposing and most disconcerting. But now he was gone she wished to tamp down her emotions.

"Oh no!" she exclaimed, shaking her head vigorously. "No, indeed, he has been most gentlemanly."

She meant it. Now she reflected back, he had been solicitous from the start, and it was just her pride and her blinkeredness which had made her push him away. How foolish he must think her now. That thought sent a horrid slither of embarrassment down into Penelope's stomach.

No doubt he thought her a silly child, just as Lady Spencer did. His kindness had likely been brought on by fraternal feeling. After all, he had not renewed his attentions since Sir Tristan's house party. Why else would he kiss her and then show no desire to want to do so again? She was a fool in his eyes.

"He is usually quite distant from Society, quiet and reserved, but he seems to—well—seek out your company."

Quiet? Reserved? That was not the man Penelope knew.

"May I..." Lady Etheridge trailed off, eyeing the handkerchief in Penelope's hands. "May I offer some advice?"

Penelope could not prevent her hackles rising. Lady Etheridge was being tremendously kind, but when people started a sentence like that, it almost always went on to contain something disagreeable. Usually concerning her father.

"I know my son has great compassion," Lady Etheridge continued gently, "and sometimes that can make him blind. My husband has concerns over your... your family history..."

There it was—the oblique reference to her father.

"And there are those lately arrived in London who are causing talk because of those whom they choose to visit. One of them, I believe, has become a friend of yours."

Gracious! Was everyone to poke their nose into Penelope's business? Didn't she have enough to contend with without Lady Etheridge acting the protective mother? Lord Standon's parent must have read this inner monologue on Penelope's face for her tone gentled.

"I know, better than my husband, that we women are hardly the mistresses of our own fate. We cannot choose the families of which we are a part. But we can choose our friendships and I would urge you to reconsider—"

"Thank you, Lady Etheridge," Penelope said, reaching over to press one of her Ladyship's hands. "You are as compassionate as your son, and he has already been good enough to deliver me of that warning, several times. He has been very conscientious in trying to aid me, but I'm afraid until now, I have been too proud to see the truth. I can assure you, I harbour none of the same beliefs as the woman of whom you speak. She is no friend of mine."

"I see my son was right when he told me how directly you speak." A little dimple appeared at the corner of Lady Etheridge's mouth. "He told me how refreshing it was in our rather verbose Society, and I'm inclined to agree."

He'd spoken of her? And was that a compliment? Perhaps Penelope's frank speech hadn't entirely insulted Lord Standon during their acquaintance.

"But I must humbly disagree with you on one point, Lady Etheridge."

"Yes?"

"I intend to be the mistress of my own fate." Penelope had no idea how she might achieve it at this moment in time. She faced an impossible situation, and could see no way out, but she had to save her family. There was no question about that. She would not give in to defeat. She *could* not. Her spirit wouldn't allow it.

Lady Etheridge's gaze was steady upon Penelope's face, and even when confronted with this sudden fierceness, it did not waver. After a moment she broke into a smile.

"I can see why my son admires you so much."

Admires? How could he admire her when she had been such a fool? Lady Etheridge must be mistaken. Perhaps he had before today, but he would do so no longer.

"I should return you to your mother," said Lady Etheridge, rising from her seat. "Are you feeling sufficiently recovered?"

"Yes, I am."

Leaving their bench, they walked to where her mother stood chatting to an old friend.

"Lady Etheridge," said Lady Harwood, after her friend bid her adieu. She inclined her head. "How nice it is to see you again so soon after our recent sojourn from London."

"I bumped into your lovely daughter, Athena. You must be proud of such an impressive young woman."

The informal greeting and compliment caused her mother's expression to soften, and Penelope saw a spark of affection in her parent's eyes.

"You are too kind, Agatha."

It was a brief hint of the friendship that had been there long ago.

They exchanged a few pleasantries and then Lady Etheridge took her leave. Penelope and her family were another hour at the exhibition, chatting to acquaintances, and Thalia enjoying the attention of her beau. But Penelope saw and heard nothing going on around her. She was entirely consumed by the threat Lady Spencer had made, and considering how best to thwart it.

CHAPTER 16

That evening they were due at the Fairings' for a recital from famed French soprano Élisabeth Duparc, but Penelope stayed home feigning a headache. Without her mother and sister present, she was able to pace the study in peace and come up with a plan.

After being thrown back and forth by her uncertain mind, Penelope had decided against telling her mother. She had already been through so much in the last few years, the last thing she needed to know was that her elder daughter had inadvertently put the whole family at risk. Nor that Lord Harwood had used her prized gift as a hiding place for Jacobite treasure.

Besides, whether her mother knew or not, the family was in danger. Either the Old Pretender's letter would be made public and ruin the Harwood name, or she would make her family party to handing back a jewel to an exiled king.

But what if the widow kept her word, and the letter remained a secret?

Surely that was the best outcome? Yet the duplicitous

behaviour of Lady Spencer up until this point made Penelope think it would not be so easy.

Even if the widow kept her word, what if the authorities got wind of the Harwoods handing over a king's ransom to the rebellious exiled king? What if it became generally known?

Penelope doubted her family's name could survive being coupled once again with the Jacobite cause. Her friendship with Lady Spencer would only compound their fate. Lady Etheridge had told her of rumours surrounding the lovers and who they were mixing with. Jacobite sympathisers. If a Society dame knew, then surely the authorities already did. Were they watching them? Were they watching Penelope?

What if she kept the clock and said nothing? Could the Harwoods weather the letter being made public?

She feared they could not. Her sister's hopes of matrimony with Lord Fairing would be dashed. They would be fortunate to be acknowledged by anyone of consequence. The family name would be destroyed.

Penelope must hand over the clock.

But what if Lady Spencer didn't keep her word?

Oh, gracious! Round in another circle. There was no way out. Penelope wished to scream.

She'd stopped again in the middle of the room, and nothing could be heard now but the crackle of the fire as she looked up at the clock on the mantel, the innocuous-looking object whose contents was tantamount to ruin.

A fitful night produced very little peace in Penelope's mind, but it did produce the resolution that she had to take the clock to Lady Spencer. She could only hope the widow's word was better than her friendship. Penelope spoke the truth when she told her mother her head still ached, and as soon as Mama and Thalia went calling, she set to her task.

She asked her maid Ginny to help her take the clock from the mantel and wrap it in a blanket, leaving the two handles free to carry it and tying the whole round with string to keep it secure.

"I will deliver this, Ginny. It must be mended. You may stay here and get on with your chores," Penelope said breezily, pulling on her gloves before fastening around her thickest cloak with the biggest hood. It was quite at odds with the weather outside.

Ginny, who had helped her mistress wrap the clock without demur, now looked quizzically at her.

"Take it to be mended, my Lady?" she asked.

As if punctuating her falsehood, the clock's loud ticks came muffled through its blanket swaddle.

"It's been running a little slow," Penelope said.

"Can I not get Joseph to look at it for you, my Lady? It'll save you the trouble of traipsing with it around London."

"No, no, I can take it. It is no bother."

"Are you well enough with your headache?"

"I shall be fine," Penelope said peevishly. "You know how Mama treasures it. She will be upset if she realises something's wrong with it, so I'm hoping to have it mended without her worrying. But I can't entrust it to anyone else."

How Penelope would explain when the clock never came back from this little trip to the 'clockmaker', she wasn't sure. That was a problem for tomorrow. For today, she had to get the clock and its contents to Lady Spencer before the woman's deadline. There would be no way for Penelope to deliver it this evening by herself without causing a great deal of talk. Now was the best time.

She pulled the hood of her cloak up and forward as far as it would go. No one would be able to see her face in this.

"Has Joseph ordered a chair?"

"Yes, my Lady, as you instructed. But I really must go with you if you are not going out with the carriage and the grooms."

"I don't think you'll be fitting in the chair with me." A chair would be unmarked, unlike the family carriage, and the fewer servants who saw where she went, the better.

"I can walk alongside it, Lady Penelope. It wouldn't be seemly for you to go without me. And you may need me."

"Ginny." Penelope took the girl's hands and looked directly in her green eyes. "I cannot explain this to you, but you may not come with me. I shall be all right, but please do not ask me any more about it."

The misgiving in the servant's face was clear, but she reluctantly obeyed her mistress and said no more on that subject. "And what shall I say then to the gentleman in the morning room?"

"Gentleman? What gentleman?"

"The gentleman who has come to call on you—did Joseph not tell you?" Ginny huffed. "I told him a quarter of an hour since, when I was off finding the string. The visitor is most insistent on seeing you. Says you have pressing business to discuss."

Count Feccio. In her impatience, Lady Spencer must have sent him to collect the clock. Penelope sighed. At least it would save an unattended trip through London and the potential for more scandal.

"Very well." She took hold of the clock's handles and hefted the heavy object off the table. "Please get the door for me, Ginny, and I shall go to him directly."

Obeying her mistress, the maid opened the door, and then after Penelope went out, she hurried past her into the hall to open the morning room door for her.

"Shall you be needing tea, my Lady?"

"No, thank you, Ginny." Penelope couldn't bring herself to look at the Count. Her heart was racing and the idea of being alone with such a man caused her blood to run cold.

She placed the clock on the table, catching sight of the

gentleman out of the corner of her eye, and turned back to her maid. "You may cancel the chair. The gentleman shall be taking the clock to be mended for me. You may leave us."

Looking as puzzled as ever, Ginny nodded at her mistress, and retreated from the room. It wasn't proper to be alone with a gentleman, but Penelope could not afford any of the servants overhearing this conversation.

Taking a deep breath, she pulled her hood down and turned to face her unwelcome visitor.

"I'm obliged to Lady Spencer for sending you to—" She broke off when she locked eyes with Lord Standon.

"Lady Penelope." He bowed and then offered her a welcoming smile. "I think you may have thought me someone else?"

"Forgive me... I did."

"I have interrupted your plans?" he asked, one questioning brow raised.

"It is no bother," she said, waving away the clock on the table as though it were nothing. His Lordship couldn't have arrived at a more inconvenient time.

"I came to see how you were after yesterday, and to conclude our conversation."

"That is very kind," Penelope replied. "Will you sit down?" She gestured to the sofa opposite while she herself took a chair.

If she humoured him for a while, reassured him that she was all right, he might leave. Perhaps she could still meet Lady Spencer's timeline without her mother or sister being any the wiser.

"And how are you this morning? I see no evidence of tears, but, if I may say so without causing offence, you do not seem your usual self either."

"You may, and you would be right," she said. "I will not

contradict you, seeing as I know you will argue the truth out of me."

He smiled. How handsome he looked when he smiled. His hazel eyes creased pleasingly at their corners and his mouth curved attractively. "We finally have an understanding."

Penelope didn't laugh despite his humour.

"You will forgive me for not being myself when I have been proven a consummate fool."

His brows rose at this and the smile disappeared. "My Lady, you are too harsh on yourself. Better an overuse of compassion than an under-use of the self-same. If that is your fault, then I think it a good one to have."

Penelope's lip wobbled involuntarily. A sudden lump appeared, unwanted, in her throat. How could this man see things so differently, yet so logically? He was immeasurably kind. Could he really not think her a fool?

"Will you tell me of your conversation with Lady Spencer —of what she demands from you?"

"No. It is nothing with which to concern yourself. All is in hand."

His eyes remained fixed on hers. Penelope felt as though he were reading her mind. Then, suddenly, he broke the gaze and said with a considerable amount of nonchalance, "I have not heard of a lady personally delivering a clock to a clockmaker— nor of a gentleman collecting one when it should be a shop boy."

The statement was uttered with no uplift in tone at the end denoting a question. Therefore Penelope chose not to deliver any kind of answer.

"May I offer you tea?" she asked, rising and walking briskly over to where the bell rope hung beside the fireplace.

"No, thank you," replied his Lordship. "What is so precious about a clock that Lady Spencer should demand it from you?"

Penelope whirled around, eyes flashing at him. "You never give up, do you?" she asked, huffing loudly. "Even when I try my best to keep you out of this horrid business."

"When it comes to you, Lady Penelope, no, I do not."

"Stop it."

"Stop what?"

"Stop looking all at ease like that and speaking so provokingly. It is no amusing matter."

"If you were to tell me what *it* is, then I may do so," he said.

There was that logic again.

Penelope came back to the chair beside him and sat with a thump. She couldn't tell him if she wished to protect him from this scandal. And yet, the idea of admitting the truth to someone else, of sharing the burden and getting help, was very appealing.

Lord Standon leant forward and reached out to place his hands gently over hers in her lap. He caressed them softly and looked coaxingly into her face.

"I do not understand why you are so insistent upon helping me," whispered Penelope, her voice cracking on the words, the urge to cry back in strength.

"If you do not understand that, Lady Penelope,"—his voice was soft and deep—"then I may have to revise my earlier statement and consider the possibility that you are being a little foolish."

"Oh!" Penelope snatched her hands away, and then seeing the gleam of mischief in his eyes and realising exactly what he was saying, chose to deal with it brusquely. "You are atrociously rude!"

The kiss they had shared at the lakeside *had* meant something to him.

But this was hardly the time to consider such things.

"Aha!" Lord Standon exclaimed. "That is better. Much

more like the Lady Penelope I have come to know. Shall we restore your nerve completely with a glass of brandy and discuss your predicament over it?"

"If you refuse to leave, I have little choice."

"Good." His Lordship rose and went over to the sideboard upon which sat a series of decanters and glasses. He poured amber liquid into two bulbous glasses and returned to the sofa, handing one to Penelope. "The whole lot—doctor's orders."

Penelope yielded, sipping the warming liquid and feeling the resultant courage after only a few minutes.

"Better. Now, out with it—why are Lady Spencer and Count Feccio after that clock, and why are you capitulating?"

Penelope took a deep breath. "The clock was a gift... it was a gift from—" Her voice dropped to a whisper. "The king over the water. He gave it to my father."

Lord Standon finished his sip and nodded, glancing over at the bundled clock which still sat on the coffee table.

"And the gift-giver wants it back?"

"That and... well... he wants what is inside it. A treasure that he left in my father's safekeeping." She was beginning to feel sick again. "Lady Spencer tried to take it when she came to visit me several days ago, but I caught her in the act."

"I see."

"I had no idea about it. I never knew my father had received such an item, I—"

Lord Standon put down his empty glass on the table and reached out to place his hands around both of Penelope's that still held her brandy glass. The action halted her panicked words.

"I understand."

The sincerity and earnest care in his eyes caused the lump to reappear in Penelope's throat, and tears to prick the backs of her eyes.

"And I presume," Lord Standon continued, "that Lady Spencer and the Count have threatened you in some way to gain your compliance?"

"There is no hiding anything from you, my Lord." One of the threatening tears had grown so large that it broke free and ran down her cheek.

He saw it and released one of her hands to gently brush away the droplet. Penelope closed her eyes, holding back further drops, and imprinting the feel of his hand into her memory.

"Tell me what she threatens?" he asked gently.

"She says if I do not deliver the clock, she will make public a most condemning letter written from the exiled king to... to my father."

She could not look him in the eye. His hand dropped from her face and her skin went cold where it had been. But to her surprise, instead of retracting from her, he took hold of both her hands again.

"I see." A minute or so passed. "I do not perceive any repercussions from delivering the clock and its contents into their hands. If it is not your family's property in the first place, it is merely returning it to its rightful owner. To keep it in Harwood House is riskier. I suppose she offers the letter in return for the treasure?"

Penelope nodded.

"Then, the only danger remains in the clock's delivery. I shall remove that danger from you by delivering it myself."

"I could not ask that of you."

"You are not asking—I am offering. Insisting, in fact. I will not leave this house until I am certain you will not be the one delivering that clock."

"I could—"

"I know you are perfectly capable of taking it yourself, of disguising your person and going secretly to Lady Spencer's abode, but I would like to take the burden from you." He pressed her hands and gazed earnestly once again into her face. "Please."

Penelope was caught in the emotion in his hazel eyes. She felt safe with him, reassured by his large, warm hands around hers, secure in his care.

"You are very kind." Two more tears fell down her cheeks.

The warmth of his hands disappeared from her own as he reached for his handkerchief.

"I am gaining a collection." She chuckled, taking the offered linen from him and dabbing at her cheeks.

Lord Standon smiled at her and then rose, taking the clock from the table. "Do you have a direction?"

Penelope nodded, rising and taking the paper with Lady Spencer's address from her pocket to hand to him.

"You're sure?" she asked.

"I'm sure, Penelope." He used her Christian name. "I shall let you know when the task is done."

A moment later, he was gone and Penelope realised he had just walked out of Harwood House with her one bargaining chip. Her whole life was in Lord Standon's hands.

CHAPTER 17

On leaving Harwood House, Roderick dispatched one of the Harwood servants to walk his horse back home and ordered a hackney. Discretion was essential.

Whatever was in this clock was worth the trouble of Lady Spencer befriending Penelope to steal it, and now to blackmail her for it. There had been no way that Roderick was going to allow Penelope to take the clock herself. The risk of carrying whatever was in it felt small compared to allowing the woman he cared for to be put in danger.

Besides, once he arrived and got hold of that letter, he fully intended on warning Lady Spencer and the Count to leave Lady Penelope alone from now on. If they had any other insidious plans towards the lady he loved, they could direct them to himself instead.

It took an excruciating three quarters of an hour to reach the widow's residence thanks to multiple carriages blocking the city roads as they unloaded passengers and goods. Enough time for Roderick's anger at Lady Penelope's two tormentors to heat and cool. So much so, that when he was ushered into a sumptuously decorated drawing room to await the mistress of the house, he was the epitome of calm.

A few minutes later, the door opened and Lady Spencer swept into the room wearing an open-fronted over-gown, unpinned, with a daring combination of petticoat and stays on full display beneath.

"Lord Standon, I hardly believed my footman when he told me it was you who had arrived with the parcel I've been waiting for. Yet here you are."

"Here I am," Roderick replied, giving the slightest of bows and refusing to look below her chin.

Through the still open door came Count Feccio, equally ill-dressed, in his shirt sleeves, with cravat missing and breeches mis-buttoned.

Roderick was more pleased than ever that he had prevented Lady Penelope from coming here. She was an innocent, and to be exposed to such licentiousness would have been shocking and humiliating.

"I have come on behalf of the lady to deliver the item you requested." He pointed to the clock he had already placed on a low rosewood table beside a chaise longue.

"I shall overlook that she disobeyed my request not to tell anyone of this transaction. To be honest, I'm a little surprised my young friend would entrust the task to anyone else. I hope telling you is her only indiscretion."

"She has not been indiscreet, Lady Spencer. I insisted on knowing the problem she faced and have offered her my aid. I am fully cognisant of the discretion required in this deal."

"They are, how do you say in English, innamorata—love —my dear." Count Feccio's lips curled into what Roderick supposed was a smile. But with his small, pointy teeth and disingenuous stare, it was hardly a generous expression on the Italian noble.

Lady Spencer laughed. "I had detected a partiality, my

Lord. I confess I thought you were going to cause me some trouble at one point. But now here you are, a little errand boy, delivering my goods." She was lacing a ribbon around her fingers which should have been tying the front of her dress together. "I did not think she reciprocated your interest, but perhaps after this little help..."

Roderick resisted the urge to roll his eyes. "Forgive me, but I was under the impression I was here to deliver this clock in accordance with your blackmail threat—not to exchange theories on Lady Penelope's preferred suitors."

"Oh, a suitor, Pascal!" Lady Spencer's eyes darted mischievously to her lover. "It is more serious than a simple tendre."

Roderick ground his teeth. He remained silent, realising quickly that whatever he said, these two were determined to have their fun.

"Come, my dear, should we not examine the gift?" Count Feccio came up behind her, massaging her shoulders, dark eyes gleaming at the clock.

Skirting around the chaise longue on which Lady Spencer had sprawled herself, the Count crouched down before the package.

"Uh-uh!" Lady Spencer snapped up from lounging and smacked his hands away viciously. "His Royal Highness gave me this mission, Pascal. *I* shall inspect it."

Roderick saw the Count shoot a venomous look at his lover before retreating to the other side of the room. Lady Spencer set to work on the knots in the string holding the bundle together. It took several minutes for her to work them loose. Her frustration was evident when she threw the untied twine across the room. It sailed through the air on an expletive and landed at the Count's feet.

Oblivious to where she had thrown it, the widow carefully unwound the blanket from the object, revealing the clock to the room. She ran long fingers over it, and then turned the face away from herself, and felt the back of the casing looking for something. Her hands paused and then she eased open a drawer at the clock's base. Aside from two music barrels, there appeared to be some kind of velvet purse inside.

He didn't have to wait long to find out what was hidden in the purse. With the flick of a finger, the clasp was undone, and then out slid the largest diamond Roderick had ever seen. It caught the light as it fell into Lady Spencer's palm and didn't seem to let it go except in a thousand tiny glittering beams that flashed across the widow's glee-filled face.

The epithet 'treasure' where this rumour was concerned was no exaggeration.

"It's as flawless as His Royal Highness described," Lady Spencer breathed, raising the stone to eye level between her forefinger and thumb and turning it slowly in the light.

"He will be pleased," said Feccio.

The widow nodded. "It will go a long way to aid his endeavours." She placed the diamond back in its pouch and looked to Roderick. "I thank you for your service. I would offer you tea, but we both know we do not wish to partake in any, so I will bid you good day."

Good day? Hang on a minute.

"I believe I am to receive a letter in exchange for that item," said Roderick steadily.

"Oh, did she tell you about that as well? Hasn't she been a noisy little bird, chirping away all these secrets?" Lady Spencer's eyes flashed unnervingly. "I'm afraid, with all these changes to our deals, I have also changed my mind." She laid back on the chaise longue, lifting up her legs onto the furniture and exposing clocked stockings. "I think I need to keep my leverage until we leave the country to make sure she doesn't decide to sing to anyone else."

"If I give you my word, as a gentleman, guaranteeing mine

and Lady Penelope's silence on the subject, will you return the letter? Or better yet, burn it?"

"I'm afraid a gentleman's word means nothing to me. I have been in Society too long for that, dear boy," said Lady Spencer. "But it is sweet of you to offer. If I see Lady Penelope again before we leave for the Continent, I shall be sure to tell her of your attempts at chivalry."

"We had a deal." Roderick stepped forward, his patience wearing thin.

Quick as a flash, the Count raised a pistol from a table behind the chaise longue and levelled it at Roderick's head.

"And the deal has changed," Lady Spencer said in light tones, smiling at Roderick's frustration. "Now please leave before the Count has to make a mess."

"Get lost, English dog," Feccio spat.

The pistol was primed, the flintlock drawn back. At this distance he wouldn't miss. Roderick only considered his options for a second before backing down.

"Then I wish you fair winds, Lady Spencer," he said as his mind sought another solution. "Perhaps—" Would that work? It was his only idea. "I may escort you to your berth and you may hand over the letter before you embark? There shall be no danger for you then, even if I were to inform the authorities. You'd be well on your way and I would have no proof of what had occurred to show them."

Lady Spencer clapped her hands together. "A cunning gentleman, aren't you, my Lord? Pascal, I do believe this man is in love. It is making him do the most foolish things."

"Love is a foolish notion," offered the Count in return, the gun not wavering.

Lady Spencer tapped a finger to the corner of her mouth as she considered Roderick's proposal.

"It is no matter to me if you wish to wave us off from this

country. Perhaps I shall feel merciful and hand it over as you suggest."

"You are too kind." Roderick bowed, his words dripping with sarcasm. The deal was not final, but he would take it. If there was any hope of protecting Lady Penelope from scandal, he had to pursue it.

"We leave tomorrow from King James' stairs. Appropriate, no?" She laughed, so pleased with her little joke.

Roderick nodded, bowed again, and took his leave. It wasn't until he was out of that scent-filled den of debauchery that he felt he could breathe again.

It was by no means clean cut. He had hoped to wash Lady Penelope's hands of this matter at the end of today. But at least there was hope for that tomorrow. Hearing these odious people threaten the woman he cared for had set his resolve. He would follow them to their berth, he would retrieve the letter, and he would save Penelope.

CHAPTER 18

D*ear P,*

My delivery was successful. However, I failed to acquire the object that requires retrieval.

I shall be travelling to where the persons in question are leaving for the Continent first thing tomorrow, and am trusting their word, that they shall hand it over before they leave.

Rest assured, I shall draw this episode to a close as swiftly as I can.

Yours

R

Penelope finished reading the letter for the third time before dropping her hand to her lap and staring out at nothing.

Lady Spencer still had the letter. She must have reneged on her deal and now Lord Standon was going to retrieve it. Should she let him go and try to get it for her?

But what if something went wrong? What if her Ladyship and the Count were being watched as Penelope had wondered, and they were arrested on their flight from the country? What if Lord Standon was there as well, and he was caught alongside them?

She couldn't allow him to risk that. But nor could she think of a way to stop him. It was late in the evening when she had received the note, and she could not send one in return without her mother hearing tell of it. It had been hard enough keeping Lady Harwood out of the study all evening so she might not discover the clock missing until this business was over.

What could she do?

There was only one thing for it. She must go to Lord Standon's residence at dawn tomorrow and gain from him the location of the rendezvous. Then she might stand him down and go herself. Yes, that's what she would do. She would go herself, and the moment she had her father's letter in her hands, she would burn it.

But to travel so early in the morning with no escort... she would need a disguise.

Dawn broke fine over London the next morning. Pale white clouds interrupted the blue-pink expanse here and there, and the morning light guided the veiled woman's progress towards Lord Standon's residence.

Seated on a fine grey, Penelope had donned one of the black mourning dresses from when her father had died, and her heavy wool cloak with the big hood. It was topped off nicely with a masquerade mask of her mother's from years ago.

She would dare anyone to guess her identity now.

The dark queen of some phantom realm—that's what she looked like. The groom had almost jumped out of his skin when he had answered her bangs on the door shortly after dawn. She'd pushed the mask up so he could recognise her before she gave him instructions to ready her mare, but still he scurried away, as though the very hounds of hell were at his heels.

At least it meant her mare was ready swiftly. No doubt there'd be gossip in the servants' hall this morning, though she had tried to swear him to secrecy. Penelope had explained she had left a note telling her mother she was urgently needed, and that time was of the essence and she must go now.

Once mounted, her heartbeat sped her along, and the further she got from the house, the less confidence she had in her disguise. She felt as though every person she passed was looking at her and was seconds away from discovering who she really was.

After what felt like an eternity, but what in actuality was half an hour, she rode into the square which had been the return address on Lord Standon's letter to her. She had already considered how she might gain entry covertly. It would hardly do for this phantom queen to be skipping up the steps of a bachelor's residence early in the morning and rapping on his door, would it?

One, two, three. She counted the houses until she came to what she knew to be Lord Standon's. The curtains were still drawn. She considered with misgiving that he may still be abed. Riding past without pause, she kept going until a break in the succession of fine Town houses signalled the entrance to the mews.

Her mare's hooves clipped excruciatingly loudly on the cobbled street around to the back of the houses, and then Penelope counted again. One, two, three... At the back of the fourth, she halted and looked up at the mishmash of old and new additions in such contrast to the uniform front that faced the square. Opposite the hodgepodge of architecture were the largely symmetrical mews, each serving the house directly before it, with housing for horses, carriages and grooms.

Relief flooded her as she saw activity in Lord Standon's stables. A lantern flickered on its hook by the door, pushing away the last vestiges of the night gloom from the stable's interior, and highlighting a groom as he strode past the doorway. He had a bridle on his shoulder, and a saddle slung over his arm, and glancing out towards Penelope he jerked to a startled halt.

"Goodness gracious!" he cried, the shock making him lose hold of the saddle.

The leather object slipped sideways on his arm, and he caught it just in time, before it went hurtling to the floor. Once it was safe, his terrified eyes again took in the ghoulish apparition before him on its ghost-white horse.

"Good morning," Penelope said, in a low voice, hoping his exclamations hadn't woken the local inhabitants. "I've come to speak to Lord Standon about the errand for which he has no doubt instructed you to saddle his horse. Would you be so good as to fetch him for me?"

"Fetch—his Lordship?" The groom was still looking at her with eyes as large as saucers.

The mask likely wasn't helping, but she could hardly remove it, could she?

"Yes, please."

"A-and who shall I say is c-calling?"

"A lady," Penelope replied. She had practised this bit in her head. "He will know who."

"A lady."

He wasn't moving.

"Yes."

Still, he remained.

"Come now, I am not here to take his soul, so if you would please hurry."

The words, though designed to calm the man, seemed to goad him into action through fear rather than reassurance. He placed the saddle and bridle on a nearby hook and half-ran to the servants' entrance at the back of the house.

Penelope waited.

Her mare shifted beneath her, no doubt smelling the hay in the stables, and wishing to be fed. Reining her backwards, hooves clipping on the cobbles, Penelope stayed the beast's fussing enough that she could look up at the surrounding houses. It wouldn't be long before the other residents of the square were awake, judging from the smoking chimneys and several open curtains. Where was that groom?

She wished to be off. The longer she waited here, the more likely she would be seen, and while she was disguised, there were no guarantees she wouldn't be recognised. She just needed the location of Lady Spencer's boat and then she could journey on by herself. The thought terrified her. But she must —she must do it.

Her mare shifted beneath her again, ears pricking and swinging her head to look round.

"And to what"—Lord Standon's voice sounded out on the quiet street—"do I owe the honour of this visit from..." He trailed off, staring up at the odd spectre. "Well—what are you? Jack please do get on and saddle my horse."

The groom, who had been skulking behind his Lordship, shot across the cobbles into the stables. He was still seemingly terrified that he might be struck down by the dark rider.

Penelope looked down at Lord Standon but was disquieted to see there was no jest in his eyes to match that of his words. He was dressed in a greatcoat, breeches and top boots, and he looked... displeased.

"I am come," Penelope said, clearing her throat, "to relieve you of your errand today. You need not be troubled by my family's scandal any further if you would be so good as to give me the direction of the berth."

"I do not think I shall."

"Please!" Penelope begged. "She should have handed over the letter, but she did not. Now your part is done, and I must see this through."

"I fear my interference made her and her friend reset the terms of the deal. Part of that was to refuse to hand over the letter. They were... most insistent on that point."

"Most insistent—what do you mean?"

"Please do not worry yourself. Just rest assured I shall not be caught off-guard again."

Caught off-guard? Had they hurt him? This was all her fault.

"I—I'm so sorry," she whispered. "I'm so ashamed of it all. I never meant for you to be put in any kind of danger from scandals that are wholly my own."

"Yours? There I must correct you most firmly, my Lady. None of this was *your* doing. And I must own my foolishness in not going armed." He was stroking her mare's neck now.

Armed? She felt sick. Instinctively she reached down, reins in one hand, so that she might touch his fingers briefly and reassure herself that he was all right.

"So we are both learning." He turned his hand over and interwove his fingers with hers as he gazed up at her. "But, your travelling here alone in that—ah—disguise, was not wise. I must adjure you to go home and allow me to retrieve the item on your behalf."

"I cannot." She pulled her hand from his, speaking louder than she intended. "Especially not now I know the danger I put you in. Surely you can see that I cannot allow you to do so. You have already done so much—too much." She retook the reins in each hand. "If you will give me the name of the place, I will be on my way."

"And if I did," said Lord Standon, leaning back on one leg and crossing his arms, "should you know which direction to go?" That infernal left brow of his rose in provoking query.

She huffed loudly. Confound the man! Forming a clear plan was a speciality of Penelope's, but this gentleman's insistence on outrageous acts of kindness interfered with her clear thinking.

"Then you shall give me directions too," she said suddenly, a look of triumph overtaking her countenance.

"I do not think I shall," he said, repeating his earlier refusal. Then, turning to the stable door, he called, "Jack, bring Tyson out."

He calmly pulled his gloves from his pocket while the groom brought his horse to stand by the mounting block. The presence of the groom prevented Penelope from making any further protestations. Lord Standon mounted, checked his girth, and gathered his reins.

"That'll be all Jack and not a word to the others, you hear? I shall make it worth your while upon my return."

"Right you are, my Lord, right you are," said the groom, tugging his forelock at his master before scurrying back to the stables.

"Are you ready?" asked his Lordship, turning to Penelope. "And before you argue with me, let me make one thing quite clear—I shall not be allowing you to face this alone, do you understand? And I will not negotiate on that."

He spoke so firmly, with such resolution, that it was all Penelope could do to maintain her composure and nod. For some unknown reason, his stubborn declaration made her wish to cry—really cry—great rolling sobs. As it was, she swallowed down the desire, and said quietly, "I'm ready."

Whether he could discern her emotions or not, in the next moment he was leaning over and squeezing her right hand on the reins.

"Have no fear, Penelope. We shall see this through, and your family will be safe."

"Yes." She really did believe him. "Lead on, my Lord."

Lord Standon smiled, retaking his reins, and set off from the mews. It was time for this scandal to be brought to its just conclusion.

CHAPTER 19

The road leading to the docks was mercifully empty of travellers at that time in the morning. Those that Roderick saw were all market traders and charwomen. There wasn't a crested carriage or sedan chair in sight.

He had supposed Penelope might find the going hard, but she made no demur, following him silently as he set a rapid pace. They must make up the time they had lost debating in the mews if they wished to catch Lady Spencer and Count Feccio before the tide.

In a little under an hour they entered the Wapping area. Gone were the genteel houses and manicured squares of the wealthy. In their place rose up practical, unbeautiful warehouses, piles of cargo—spices, tobacco, tea and silk—and rough men getting to their day's work. Plenty of those about stared at the veiled woman, riding like some mythological goddess of the underworld, through their streets. They made no attempt at concealing their interest as they dropped their activities to gawp as she rode past.

At least, Roderick mused, they had no hope of recognising her in that disguise. And he was not known in these parts. Beyond him being a gentleman, as denoted by his clothes, that was all they would know. A gentleman and his phantom.

The couple trotted some way along the main thoroughfare, the morning air cold and damp, and a mist from the Thames creeping up from the various watermen's stairs—the narrow passageways that snaked between the buildings and gave access to the river. He read the signs of each as they passed, looking for the name Lady Spencer had given him. Frying Pan stairs, New Crane stairs. Each gave a glimpse of the Thames with its murky water—the lifeblood of London.

Turning right to keep on the main road through the docks, they passed two more side streets, but these led to boatyards rather than the river. Already workers gathered in them for the day ahead. Then he saw it—a chaise and four pulled up beside an opening between the buildings, and up there on the wall the sign read, King James' stairs.

He hardly needed the confirmation of the sign. The smartly painted chaise stuck out like a sore thumb. Reining in his mount, he waited for Penelope to draw alongside him.

"That's their carriage. Their boat will be down there." He nodded to the narrow alley that led to the water.

"They're leaving London from *here*?" asked Penelope, dismay in her voice.

"They are no doubt wishing to avoid notice. I suspect they have a berth on a merchant ship."

"I see," she replied.

A breeze sprang up from the river and Roderick saw her shiver. The colour had drained from her face.

"You do not have to come."

"Yes, I do. It's my family's mess and I must face it."

Before he could dismount and offer her his assistance, she had taken her foot from the stirrup, swung her leg over the horn, and was sliding easily to the ground.

Following suit, wondering if he would ever be able to keep up with this woman, he looked for a place to tether the horses.

"There," he said in a low voice, pointing to a stack of cargo lashed together with ropes. Roderick led the way over, and they tied each of their horses' reins to the ropes. Turning back to Penelope, he saw her locking and unlocking her fingers from each other and immediately reached out and took one of her hands, placing it firmly on his arm and squeezing it tight.

"Let's end this business."

Penelope nodded, and they approached the watermen's stairs.

Penelope couldn't stop shivering. The damp wind coming up off the river didn't help, but she would have been lying to herself if she said that was the only cause.

Approaching the chaise and four, she spied the driver, standing at his horses' heads. He eyed the newcomers suspiciously. Lord Standon ignored the servant, so Penelope followed suit, chin raised, gaze resolutely on the alley that led to the river.

Never having been to such a part of London before, her heart was beating double speed. The muck, the gruff workers, the dark dirtiness of it all. How grateful she was not to be alone.

"Down here." Lord Standon turned back at the top of the stairs to offer a helping hand to Penelope. She took it without argument and together they began to descend.

The warehouses and boat stores either side of King James' stairs gave way in the centre to a dual set of stairs running alongside one another. The set on the right ran higher than the left, breaking in the middle with a flat landing, before descending once again. It was upon this landing that a pile of trunks and valises sat, and they were being ferried further down the stairs, one at a time, to where a small boat was moored waiting, its bow right up against where the lower set of stairs rose out of the water.

Alongside the pile of luggage stood its owners, Lady Spencer and Count Feccio. The silk and fine cut of their clothes sat ill against the backdrop and they were chattering away, laughing, as the men worked diligently around them. Penelope saw Count Feccio's arm around Lady Spencer's waist and he laid a kiss upon her neck as she laughed.

"I can do the talking if you wish?" said Lord Standon, holding Penelope steady as they descended the uneven steps.

Lady Spencer laughed again, loudly, the sound grotesque as it bounced off the water and back up the stairs.

A flash of anger briefly eclipsed Penelope's nerves.

"I should like to," she whispered, far more quietly than she intended.

Lord Standon nodded just as they were hailed from below.

"We have a farewell party to see us off," cried Count Feccio. It was his turn to laugh now.

Lady Spencer turned around, her face as beautiful as ever, looking strangely gleeful against the brown of the water and the surly faces of the men who loaded the boat.

"Ah, and we have both the little lovebirds."

Lord Standon and Penelope came to a stop a few steps above the leaving pair.

"Good morning," said Penelope, wishing to tell Lady Spencer to be quiet, but refraining for the moment. "The letter, if you please."

"Gracious, but you are solemn. Surely it has been amusing to disguise yourself in that silly outfit and ride across London without a chaperone? Tell me you have not had a little fun?" White teeth flashed as the widow grinned up at them. "Doesn't she look dramatic, Pascal?"

"Dreadfully so. The poor child—she fears for her reputation," her lover replied.

"So she should. Tut, tut, tut, my child." Lady Spencer wagged a gloved finger mockingly at Penelope, grinning all the more as she did so. "I am surprised at you—such a risk. But then again, I should probably do the same if I had such a dangerous secret to keep safe." The widow reached back into the fur muff she held and withdrew the letter.

"Give it to me," Penelope demanded.

"Uh-uh! Patience, my child, patience."

"I am afraid," Lord Standon cut in, "we do not derive the same pleasure from the sound of your voice as you do, Lady Spencer. So if you would be so good as to fulfil your part of the deal, and hand over the letter to my companion, I'd be grateful."

Penelope froze. Simultaneously exultant at the superbly delivered set-down, and fearful of its repercussions.

To her surprise, however, Lady Spencer burst out laughing again, the sound grating.

"My, you are smitten, aren't you?"

One of the watermen whispered something to the Count.

"My dear, we are loaded and ready to go. We must get aboard to catch the tide."

Her Ladyship sighed and shrugged. "I am afraid we must go—it's been a pleasure, Lady Penelope."

"I cannot say the same," Penelope shot back.

"Farewell." Lady Spencer turned, letter still in hand, to descend the last few steps and be handed into the ferry boat.

"You promised!" cried Penelope.

At that moment, Lord Standon stepped in front of her and from the folds of his greatcoat, drew a cocked pistol.

"My turn, Feccio," said his Lordship coolly.

The Italian noble had been about to follow after his lover, but the barrel of the gun jerked him to a stop.

"If you would be so good as to ask your lady to hand over the letter."

Feccio gulped, the sound audible.

"Louisa." The widow's Christian name came out like a rodent's squeak.

"I don't think she can hear you over the waters, Feccio. A little louder, if you please." Lord Standon flicked the muzzle of the gun upward purposefully, before levelling it at Feccio's chest again.

"Louisa!" Feccio screamed, eyes wild and spittle flying. "Louisa! For goodness' sake, give them the cursed letter."

Penelope stared out from behind Lord Standon, observing Feccio near to tears, and Lady Spencer standing on the ferry boat's deck behind him.

The widow rolled her eyes. "Do stop whining, Pascal!"

"Please, Louisa, just give it to them."

Lady Spencer tapped the letter to the corner of her mouth, clearly considering if the death of her lover was worth the possession of the letter. The longer she waited, the closer Feccio got to sobbing.

"I suppose you are no further use to the cause now," she said at last. "So this piece of paper is useless to us. You can have it. Pascal, give it to them."

Lord Standon nodded an agreement for Feccio to descend the last few steps and reach out across the water for the letter.

"Quickly, if you please. My finger is getting tired on this trigger."

Feccio was scowling up at Lord Standon and Penelope when he turned around with the letter in his hand. Penelope stepped out from behind Lord Standon and reached for the letter.

Just as she was about to grasp it between her fingers, Feccio threw it, turning and leaping from the steps into the boat.

Penelope jumped to catch the letter. Losing her footing, she plunged backwards, missing the flying paper. But it was not hard stone she fell on. It was soft, warm, and strong.

By the time she realised what had happened and looked down again towards the water, Feccio had righted himself on the boat and Lady Spencer was cursing him as the ferry disappeared from view around the buildings.

"Are you alright?" asked Lord Standon from beneath her.

She realised then that his left arm was around her, preventing her from falling off the high steps into the water below.

"The letter. Why did I try to catch it? The river will destroy it just as well."

"It would, but as it is, *I* caught it." He raised his left hand from her body and within his grasp was the letter.

"Oh!" The emotions raging through Penelope, chief among them relief, overwhelmed her defences and she burst into tears. "Oh, th-thank you."

Lord Standon's arms wrapped around her and held her tightly to him as he murmured reassurances into her ear.

"Penelope, please don't cry," he murmured after a time, brushing her hair from her face. In falling, her mask had been thrown back and was tangled somewhere in her hair. "All is well now, and it wounds me to see you upset."

Those beautiful words stilled her sobbing. She rose up from his chest, his arms immediately releasing her.

"Have we done something terrible in letting her have the diamond?"

"I have already considered that. We will inform the revenue men. She won't get far."

"You have thought of everything," said Penelope, looking down and eyeing the gun still in his hand. Lord Standon noted her gaze and uncocked the gun, placing it back in his greatcoat pocket.

"It was rather funny to see Feccio screaming like that." Penelope giggled, unable to stop herself. The awful scene they had just witnessed replayed vividly in her mind and she immediately felt the inappropriateness of her action. "Lady Spencer was so beastly. How could anyone be like that? I just can't understand it."

"Because you are kind, dear Penelope, and she is not. Now don't think of her anymore." He brushed her wild hair away again, tucking it behind her ear, and stroking her cheek. She shivered.

"Are you cold?"

She shook her head.

He ran his thumb over her bottom lip. His eyes dropped to follow the movement. But as if remembering himself and exactly where they were—tangled up on a watermen's stairs—he shook himself.

"Come, we must get you home, my Gothic queen."

He hoisted them both up and then pressed the letter into her hands. "For your safekeeping."

She took it—the small innocuous-looking piece of paper that had almost ended her family's good name—and pushed it deep into one of her pockets beneath her cloak.

They ascended the stairs once more, retrieved their mounts from where they'd tied them, and left Wapping in their wake. As they rode back through London, Penelope could not stop the early morning events replaying in her mind. Nor could she forget the feel of Lord Standon's arms around her, his steady frame beneath her, or the thumb that had run across her lip.

CHAPTER 20

R oderick led them directly back to Harwood House. It was nearing ten o'clock and Polite Society was waking up. The likelihood of being seen was increasing and taking her back to his own abode was out of the question.

As they turned into Curzon Street, leading to Berkeley Square on which Harwood House was situated, Roderick caught sight of a carriage drawn up at one of the residences. His stomach dropped. The last thing they needed was someone descending the steps of their house as Roderick and a phantom woman rode by.

"Come to my right side," he called back softly.

Penelope obeyed, urging her mare forward. It was the best he could do to obscure her, though there was no telling who might be peering out their window.

"I have never been gladder you chose such a disguise," he murmured across at her. "Did I tell you it was a stroke of genius?"

"No, but I thank you for the compliment. That is the Leightons' house."

They were level with the carriage now. Roderick purposefully avoided eye contact with the groom standing at the horses' heads.

"The front door is still shut. We may safely hope they have not come out yet." The tension melted away from Roderick's shoulders. "Thank you, God, for that mercy. To fail at the final hurdle would have been devastating indeed. But let us hurry." He urged his horse to quicken its pace.

They were past the Leightons' residence now, without seeing a member of the household, and finally turned into Berkeley Square.

"I have never been happier to see home," said Penelope.

"Nearly there."

They made quick work of the last hundred yards, Roderick praying the neighbours rose late, and turned off down the side street into the mews. Penelope pointed out the Harwood stables, and they reached them in a matter of seconds.

"Safe," Roderick said, more to himself than his companion, and reined in his horse before dismounting. He tied the beast to a nearby hook and turned to help Penelope down.

She slipped her foot from her stirrup and slid happily into Roderick's waiting arms. His hands found her waist, holding her fast, and when she reached the floor, he pressed himself against her.

"Well, Lady Penelope," he said, wishing her mask were not obscuring her beautiful face. "You have led me on quite the adventure."

She tipped her chin up, eyes large and gaze soft upon his own, her plump lips parted a little.

"I should like to—" Roderick started.

Someone cleared their throat.

Penelope reared back in Roderick's arms and both turned to where, not a groom, but Lord Fairing stood glaring at them from beneath thunderous brows.

"Good morning, Lord Standon." He bowed stiffly. "And I *presume* Lady Penelope."

The man was blushing. Furiously. Roderick resisted the urge to laugh.

"You presume right, my Lord," Roderick replied. "I was just escorting Lady Penelope back inside."

Lord Fairing made a sound akin to a horse snorting. "I came to deliver a bouquet for when Lady Thalia arises and did not wish to disturb the household by ringing at the front door. Had I known... Lady Penelope, do you wish me to escort you back inside?"

The man clearly thought Roderick was taking advantage of the woman at his side. Had Lord Fairing seen the look of invitation on Penelope's face just now, he wouldn't have harboured such fears.

"Thank you, my Lord," said Penelope, nervously. "But I'm happy for Lord Standon to do so. Though I must thank you for your kindness to my sister in bringing her flowers."

Lord Fairing made a different sound this time. A self-deprecating growl.

"Good day to you." He bowed again, stiffly as ever, his brows raised in a supercilious fashion as he gave them one last glare before striking out in a swift walk down the mews and around the corner into the square.

"I think I may need to call on Lord Fairing to impress upon him the importance of discretion, and to allay any fears he has over your family's lack of propriety, for the sake of your sister."

"Thank you," Penelope said with feeling.

Roderick turned back to her and felt the strongest urge to kiss those lovely lips, but refrained. There was no sense chancing things now.

"Come, let's get you inside before any more of your sister's suitors spot us." He saw disappointment flash across her face.

Ushering her up the back steps and into the house, he was surprised to find all was not as sleepy as Lord Fairing's words had led them to believe. A woman was shouting. Lady Harwood, in fact. It was not until they had made it up the backstairs and into the hall that Roderick could make out what she was yelling.

"What do you mean Lady Penelope gave the clock to a gentleman?"

Something crashed against the door and rolled out onto the hall floor. A blotter.

"I am sorry your Ladyship, but—"

"And you cannot tell me where she has gone this morning?" Lady Harwood's voice was becoming hysterical. "Her note does not say!"

"My mother," Penelope said, rushing forward. "I must go to her."

She walked fearlessly through the dangerous doorway into the study and Roderick followed suit. They were presented with a scene of carnage.

Lady Harwood paced beside a Chinese cabinet, the doors open and the furniture's contents strewn across the floor surrounding it. On the other side of the room, a bureau had received similar treatment.

"Mama," Penelope cried, running to her mother and taking her flailing hands in her own. "Mama, please, it's all right. I am here."

"Penelope! Where have you been? Where is your father's clock? You must tell me. You know it was your father's gift to me. I cannot bear the thought of it not being in this house."

"Mama, calm down, please. It's all right. I have... something's happened... it's—"

"Lady Harwood, if you allow me, I will explain," Roderick said, taking command of the room. "But first, I believe this is a matter that must be discussed in private." He turned to the housekeeper who stood nearby, having tried in vain to calm her mistress before their arrival.

"It's all right, Mrs Hughes," said Penelope. "Please leave us." She ushered the housekeeper from the room, shutting the door behind her.

Roderick went to the sideboard and poured a generous glass of brandy, bringing it to Lady Harwood. "A large swig, please, and then I will begin."

Her Ladyship looked with bewilderment between her daughter and Roderick.

"Lord Standon… " She murmured, allowing her daughter to lead her to a chair, and then accepting the drink from Roderick.

Once she had taken two large gulps, he began, starting from the beginning, explaining the whole. With every twist and turn, the shock reached new levels on Lady Harwood's face.

"It was all my fault, Mama," Penelope cut in after Roderick had spoken of the blackmail. "I thought I was helping, but I was a fool."

"You were compassionate," Roderick corrected. "It appears the widow has been acting for the Old Pretender, desiring to retrieve the treasure hidden inside the clock he gifted to your husband for safekeeping."

"The clock?" Lady Harwood looked dazed. "But it was your father's gift to me."

Penelope watched the realisation and the subsequent pain work its way across her mother's features. She took a long draught of brandy and was silent for a full minute before speaking again.

"I thought I knew the name Spencer," she said faintly. "Your father used to speak about her late husband, years ago."

"From my enquiries, she is a known figure at the court in exile. Your daughter, in a brave attempt to save your family from further scandal, took it upon herself to deliver the clock and its contents to Lady Spencer. On learning of her intentions, however, I insisted on delivering the item. We did so, but there was a letter which Lady Spencer held as security until we retrieved it this morning, before she set sail for the Continent."

On cue, Penelope pulled the letter from her pocket and handed it to her mother. Lady Harwood took it and unfolded the paper, reading the contents, her face going white.

"How could he have been so foolish?" she whispered. Neither Penelope nor Lord Standon intimated that they had heard. "I always feared these conspiracies would come back to haunt us."

"Please do not concern yourself." Roderick interjected before Lady Harwood could fret further. "I will inform the revenue officers who may be able to catch Lady Spencer and her accomplice Count Feccio in the Channel. It should be easy enough to keep the Harwood name out of it, thanks to them courting so many Jacobite sympathisers while they were in England. The only thing which remains to connect you with the Stuart cause is that letter." He pointed to it.

"And I know exactly where this needs to go." Penelope rose, pulling the letter from her mother's hands and throwing it onto the fire which was warding off the morning chill.

She remained there, staring at the paper while the flames licked around it, curled it up, turned it black and then to ash. All three of them watched the final shred of danger disappear before their very eyes.

"I am so sorry," said Lady Harwood quietly.

Roderick saw tears on her Ladyship's face.

"I never meant for this to happen. Your father made me promise to keep the clock to remember him by when he died. If I had known what it contained..."

"I know, Mama," replied Penelope gently. "None of us

knew."

Lady Harwood rose and embraced her daughter. The moment, so poignant and intimate, caused Roderick to silently move over to the window to give them privacy.

After a few moments and some quietly spoken words between mother and daughter, Lady Harwood called over to him.

"And how, Lord Standon, shall I ever repay your kindness towards my daughter?"

"Do not thank me yet," Roderick replied, "for I failed to keep our activities this morning a complete secret. Lord Fairing saw us arrive just now when he was delivering flowers for Lady Thalia."

"I do not care what he thinks!" said Penelope defiantly.

"Thalia will care," said her mother. "If he chooses to say anything, he may cause a scandal, and he will most certainly retract his suit for your sister's hand."

"Agreed. I will call upon him directly," said Lord Standon.

"And you, my Lord." Lady Harwood stepped forward to bar his exit from the room. "Can you be trusted? Your father's dislike of our family is hardly a secret."

Roderick considered her words and decided this was the moment he had been waiting for.

"Perhaps I may allay your fears and remove this indiscretion in Lord Fairing's eyes in one fell swoop."

He had a feeling her words had been intentionally provoking, for she was smiling at him.

"I see," said Lady Harwood, a knowing look in her eyes.

He could not help but respond in kind, smiling back. Then the two of them turned towards Penelope, whose brow was wrinkled adorably in her attempt to follow the conversation.

"How can you do that?" Penelope asked.

"Why, by marrying you, my Lady."

CHAPTER 21

"I think I should leave you both to talk."

Penelope's stomach clenched as her mother opened the study door.

"But Mama!" Her mind was still reeling at Lord Standon's words.

Lady Harwood ignored her pleas and murmured something to Lord Standon before leaving the room. The moment the door was shut, Penelope could no longer hold her tongue.

"I shan't marry you just because you must do so to save my reputation." She began pacing, glaring repeatedly at him each time she turned in his direction. "I won't, I tell you."

"I believe you," he said calmly. "But perhaps I may assure you, that my desire to marry you—yes, *desire*—does not come from any demand of propriety."

He came over to interrupt her path, forcing her to halt and look up at him.

"I think I have been clear, but I am happy to be clearer still. I love you, Penelope."

"Oh!" She wrung her hands, eyes slipping from his face, and she turned away to pace again. "You are—you are—oh! I do not know what you are! You make me quite a mess and I have no idea why you should love me."

"I know, I'm intolerable," Lord Standon said with a chuckle.

"No!" she cried, turning back to him, her blue eyes all softness. "You are not! You are kind, and selfless and good. I don't deserve such kindness when I have been so silly."

Roderick raised a hand in a gesture to stop her. "Please don't speak of yourself in such a fashion. You did what you thought was right with the information you had. In fact, you acted with more compassion, generosity of spirit and courage than I have seen in any other woman I've come across. I wish to marry you, Penelope, because I have never met anyone like you before and I don't think I ever will again. If I do not ask you to be my wife, I shall live to regret it forever."

Such words! Such beautiful words! She could not believe her ears. This gentleman—so kind and good and honourable —loved her. He had cared for her, protected her, even when she had fought it. She had never felt as safe as when she was in his arms.

"And I should regret it," she said, a shy smile upon her lips, "if I said no."

Roderick's face broke into a grin, and he came forward, taking her into his arms, and holding her close. The feel of his strong arms around her, the breadth of his chest, and his musk, it sent her mind and body whirring. He cupped her head to his chest, squeezing her tight, and then drew back so that he might kiss her.

His lips against hers were soft and gentle, showing her how he loved her. And she responded, sensations of pleasure sparking under her skin as she spoke back in the same physical language of love.

"You feel perfect in my arms," he murmured against her lips.

"But—" Penelope's head was swimming with emotion, yet through it, reality peeked its unwelcome head. "What if Lord Fairing is not convinced by our engagement?"

"I have no cause for concern in that quarter. I've never seen the dull dog so enamoured with anyone as he is with your sister. I have no doubt I can convince him to become my brother-in-law."

"Oh good." Penelope nodded, the frown still in place on her brow as she wracked her brains for any other loose ends that required tying up.

"And what of your father?"

"He shall come round—likely when he realises you are not a Catholic convert as he suspects of all your family. I believe you have already won over my mother. Now, my darling." Roderick released her waist so that he might cup her face in both his hands. "May I request a respite from that quick mind of yours and ask that we repose instead in our newly betrothed bliss?"

Penelope's lips curved into a delighted smile.

"Yes, of course... Roderick," she said, testing out his name.

"Never has my name sounded better. Now,"—he pulled her into his arms again—"where were we?"

He dropped his lips to hers, gently brushing her skin, before kissing her passionately once more.

The End

REVIEW THIS BOOK

Thank you for reading *A Time for Scandal*.

If you enjoyed it, please share your review on Amazon, BookBub or Goodreads to help other readers find my book.

GLOSSARY

Bach - full name Johann Sebastian Bach, was a German composer and musician in the late Baroque period.

Battle of Preston - took place on 9-14 November, 1715 and was the final action of the Jacobite rising of 1715, an attempt to put James Francis Edward Stuart on the British throne in place of the Hanoverian George I.

Bergère hat - a woman's hat in a shepherdess style. Usually made of straw with a shallow crown and a wide brim.

Casaquin - a hip-length, fitted coat, worn over a matching petticoat as a fashionable women's ensemble, popular in France and Italy. It was the predecessor to the popular *Pet en L'air* of the mid and later 18th century.

Chaise longue - a sofa designed for reclining with an arm only on one end.

Élisabeth Duparc - was a French soprano who performed in several of Handel's oratorios and operas.

Engageates - false sleeves, often ruffles or flounces of layered lace, tacked to the end of elbow-length sleeves to provide a decorative edging.

Ennui - a feeling of listlessness and dissatisfaction arising from a lack of occupation or excitement.

Gilflurt - a proud minx; a vain or capricious woman.

Glorious Revolution - in 1688, a combination of nobles, politicians and churchmen wrote to William of Orange to ask him to take the throne of England from the Catholic James II (House of Stuart) as fears of a re-Catholicising of England had gripped the nation. William was James' nephew and married to James' daughter Mary. Both were Protestant. James II was deposed and replaced by William III & Mary II of England, Ireland & Scotland. It marked the beginning of a constitutional monarchy, but the deposed James II and his descendants in the House of Stuart continued to pose a risk to the throne well into the 18th century.

Hanoverian - the House of Hanover is a European royal house with roots in the Holy Roman Empire.

Hartshorn - smelling salts derived from the horns of red deer.

Jacobite (ism) - a political ideology advocating the restoration of the House of Stuart to the British throne.

Knight and barrow pig - more hog than gentleman. A saying of any low pretender to precedency.

Letter - Lord Harwood's letter from the Old Pretender in Chapter 13 is based on a real letter written by James Francis Edward Stuart to Simon Fraser, 11th Lord Lovat dated 3rd May 1703.

Lappets - a decorative flap or hanging as part of a headdress, often two long strips of lace hanging from the top of the head at the back, down over the shoulders.

Mantua - a gown, typically worn over stays and a stomacher, popular from the 1670s onwards. The mantua was generally made from a single length of fabric and pleated to shape with a train that could be pinned back to show the material to advantage.

Old Pretender - the name for James Edward Francis Stuart, son of James II and claimant to the throne from 1701 until his death in 1766.

Over the water - a euphemism used when referring to the Old Pretender. One would say, 'the king over the water' because he was exiled.

Paper-skulled - a thin skulled, foolish fellow.

Periwig - the full name to describe a styled headdress made of false hair and from which the word 'wig' is taken.

Polite Society - during the 18th century, politeness became an ideology and the way of the higher social classes to distinguish themselves from the rising middle classes. The term Polite Society referred to that high social set.

Revenue officer/men - officials given the responsibility to stop the smuggling of goods to avoid taxation.

Robe volante - a loose, unwaisted dress which hung pleated from the shoulder over hoops. It originated in 18th century France.

Rotten Row - a broad avenue through Hyde Park in London commissioned by William III to travel safely between Kensington and St James' Palace. It was called Route du Roi, French for King's Road, which was eventually corrupted to 'Rotten Row'. This avenue became popular in the 18th century for the upper classes to be seen walking or riding.

Serpentine - a forty-acre recreational lake in Hyde Park created in 1730 at the request of Queen Caroline.

Sheriffmuir - an engagement in the 1715 Jacobite rising.

Stays - a predecessor to the corset, stays were usually made of a heavy-weight material and had boning for structure. They were laced either front, back, or both and had adjustable straps to get the desired fit. They would be worn over a chemise.

Stuart - the House of Stuart was a royal house in Scotland and later Great Britain.

Sweetmeats - sugar covered fruit or nuts.

Tragedienne - an actress who specialised in tragic roles.

Tête-à-tête - a private conversation between two people.

Young Pretender - the name for Charles Edward Stuart, son of the Old Pretender and claimant to the throne from 1766 until his death in 1788. He was also known as the Young Chevalier and Bonnie Prince Charlie.

WANT TO BE IN THE KNOW?

Be the first to know about freebies, sales and when Philippa's next book releases by signing up to her newsletter.

Sign up below:

philippajanekeyworth.com/newsletter

FREE CHAPTER

Ladies of Worth, book 1

Chapter 1

London, England 1774

"Are you always so demanding?" asked Lord Avers, smiling saucily and flashing his white teeth as he gave up a card to the player beside him.

"Always," replied Angelica Worth, turning from the retreating waiter she had ordered to do her bidding and plucking a card from the table with her small, sprite-like fingers. Her blue eyes glinted as they ran over the cards in her hand. "I like to have my own way," she said simply, preparing for her last lay, "even if it is detrimental to my circumstances." She extracted some cards from her hand and placed them on the table. "In this case, it is not."

As she leant, far from innocently, across the table and draped her elegant hands across her winnings, she was greeted by a cacophony of groans. Players threw down their cards, the game over, but not one failed to notice the pale white bosom of the female gamester. Angelica knew what she was doing. Of course she did. This was not the first time she had gamed in a hell, and it was not the first time she had won from these men. Let them stare, let them imagine, let them fantasize about the woman they thought a harlot. If it distracted them enough to forget they had lost to her, to play her again, and to lose again, then all the better.

"Alas, in this case it is to *my* detriment," said Lord Avers, still put out by his loss.

Angelica returned the saucy smile he had given her earlier. A delicate crease appeared at the corner of her mouth, causing the patch near her red lips to lift teasingly. Her light blue eyes gave him a coquettish look, and she parted her lips to reveal a hint of her white teeth.

At this display of her charms, Lord Avers' face softened. It always worked—the hint of suggestion and those feminine wiles with which she could even the odds in a male-dominated arena.

A waiter appeared, offering Angelica a glass full of amber-coloured liquid on a mock-silver tray. She took a sip, the sweet orange-flower Ratafia leaving honey-like trails down her throat. She rarely drank, especially whilst gaming, but this evening was at an end and she deserved it. By the sheer exercise of her wits, she had dragged her household out of the financial gutter it had dug itself into over the last month. She would drink now and enjoy these short hours of respite before more money needed to be won.

In the brief quiet while she sipped her drink, she forgot about the staring Lord Avers and glanced over her glass rim at John Williams, the servant she always brought with her. He stood at the far wall, blending into the mahogany with his brown woolen frock coat. If he had been a more noticeable person, he might have looked out of place, but he was the kind of man who was invisible. That was why Angelica brought him, as her protection, as a sort of bodyguard-come-chaperone, if a bastard female gamester could have one of those. All she asked of him was that he stand by while she gamed for hours. He would say nothing, do nothing, but his presence would inevitably calm her, and she always received his company gratefully on the dark, early-morning journeys home. John acknowledged her look with a brief glance and then resumed his study of the middle distance.

"You know," mused Lord Avers, watching the card dealer clear the table which was now empty of players, "I think you some kind of witch. You fly in, you take my money, and I am all the happier for it." His brown eyes were the sort a woman could get lost in, his smile the kind that would melt a heart of ice. But Angelica Worth was not interested in getting lost, and her past had more than hardened her heart. She had come to Town for one reason, a reason that would not be served by an illicit liaison.

She laughed suddenly, the action lighting up her often-serious countenance. "You flatter me, my lord." And it was real flattery. She was quite aware of the sway Lord Avers held over the marriage mart with his dashing good looks. She had watched him, in another time, at another place, as another person, captivate many a woman who afterwards set their cap at him.

Unfortunately for her, Lord Avers was the third son of the Duke of Mountefield, destined to play his life out as an officer in the army with no larger financial prospects. And for Angelica's alter-ego, the full daughter of her father, her real self whom she played during the day, such a match would be impossible. Miss Caro Worth—a respectable woman who would have no more to do with gaming than she would a low-cut dress—would not spend the rest of her life trailing after his Majesty's army, no matter how beautiful the eyes of the man.

"I had rather catch you than flatter you, O Beauteous Wood-Nymph." Lord Avers' fingers brushed across Angelica's, halting them from tracing a pattern over her empty glass.

Angelica's body stiffened then. She was not Miss Caro Worth this evening, and Lord Avers was not a potential husband here. It left a bitter taste in her mouth, the knowledge of whom she played on these dark nights and of the values she let slip so easily through her fingers. She was merely a bastard gamester of no virtue in these haunts. She was not scared by his touch, but she was no fool either. She trod a dangerous line in this precarious world. That was why she had rules. That was why she was always aloof, always superficially charming, but always a foot away from everyone.

She noted the movement John made at the side of the room, treading closer in reaction to Lord Avers' touch. She shot him a quick look to make him stay where he was and then slipped her hand out from beneath Lord Avers' caress.

Her coy smile resurfaced. "If you were to catch me, my lord, I am afraid my magic would be lost. Is that not the way of phantoms or magic beings? We are not for catching but for admiring." Her full lips curved up on one side, her stomach tight as she waited for his response.

Lord Avers eyed the heart-shaped patch so coquettishly placed. He sighed, resigning himself to the fate of all Angelica's would-be lovers. He threw up a hand, the gold embroidery of his cuff catching the candlelight. "Very well, I will content myself with looking."

She breathed easier then, her spirit greatly relieved but also a little deflated. That roguish smile appealed to Angelica in spite of her rules. If she did not have a plan, one that required strict adherence, she would have said she liked Lord Avers. She had played with him several times, and he was not tinged with the same competitive desperation as many others.

He turned away from Angelica, looking for his next game as she would be doing tomorrow night. For now, she must deposit her winnings.

Angelica rose and gathered her takings. Then, swinging her full skirt round, she traversed the gaming tables. The hell was full tonight, the air lying thick between the gentlemen as they played. The dark panelling of the establishment only added to the feeling of vice as the darkness shunned in other places bred excitement in the hell.

As she looked about her, she saw the usual gamers scattered across the card room. Sir Denby, Mr. Ashby, and Lord Maltravers were at piquet a short distance away. Mr. Went was playing whist with Sir Percy and two other gentlemen. Lord Fitzhubert and the Earl of Bevenshire had just now arrived. Those were the notables; they were interlaced with other persons and personages less important to Angelica—gamers without the deep pockets she wished to plunder.

The candlelight half-shadowed the faces of the players, the dimness masking their concentration, despair, or triumph. Other faces, those watching the play, were animated by conversation and liquor, and still others keenly scanned the room for the few ladies present.

Angelica herself attracted attention at each table she passed. She had only been in Town a year, and the presence of a bastard female gamester, one who had gained admission to the hells through her aristocratic father's soiled connections, had intrigued gentlemen young and old.

She had known it would, and she had helped in that regard by refusing to powder her dark hair and thus making herself stand out from any other woman of fashion. She was not averse to attention, as long as she could control it. Society enjoyed a scandal—she had firsthand experience of this—and if she could give it a scandal of her own devising, then she cared naught for what was said.

For now, she ignored the scattered glances and stares she evoked by her passage, confirming her position as the untouchable gamester Angelica Worth, too haughty, too aloof, too distant to approach. She passed a group of revelers just arrived through the two bolted doors guarding the hell's entrance, and made her way to where Mr. Russell, the proprietor of the establishment, stood. He nodded to her.

"Good evening, Mr. Russell." She inclined her head to the short, stout man.

"Good evening Miss Worth." Mr. Russell's neat little wig bobbed just below her nose. "I see you had luck on your side at tonight's play?"

"You are correct, Mr. Russell. May I use your private rooms for a few moments?"

"But of course." Mr. Russell reached into his waistcoat and fished out a long golden chain—the line appeared never-ending until the soft, light tinkle of a key could be heard as it popped over the edge of his pocket.

He escorted her through the double doors opposite, into a room set out for hazard and other games of chance that Angelica had never played, until he came upon a hidden door, paneled just as the wall was, barely noticeable in the dim light. She could hear the slide of the lock drawing back, and then Mr. Russell's short legs trotted to the side so that she might enter. She dropped several coins in his hand as she passed. He gave no acknowledgement that he had received them other than closing the door behind her.

A small library opened up before her, the candles lit in the sconces casting a warm glow over the whole room. Books lined two of the walls, or—as Angelica knew from previous visits to this room—what might better be described as a façade of books. Mr. Russell was aware of the environment in which his clients enjoyed relaxing, but he would not spend his hard-earned money lining shelves with expensive volumes.

Angelica moved forward, the wide hips of her *robe à la française* twisting and turning between the small table and the two wingback chairs while avoiding the fire that burned merrily in the hearth. For the first time since she had entered the hell this evening, she breathed deeply. This was the moment she longed for each night that she entered Mr. Russell's establishment—the moment when she felt the relief of financial pressures, the moment when she received respite from the role circumstances demanded she play, the moment when she could prepare for her homeward journey and the sleep stolen from her by her nocturnal profession.

She had never been robbed, but as a woman travelling in this world of men, she could not risk losing the precious money she won. Her first lot of winnings had gone to Mr. Russell to ensure he spread the rumour that she kept her winnings in his private rooms and sent for them at a later date. The rumour worked well. Only he knew that she took them with her each night, and he would not tell anyone, not after the money she had paid him and continued to pay him.

She ran an unthinking hand over the spines of the false books and sighed. She was tired tonight, ready for the evening to end. When she came to the final column of books, near the far corner of the room, she stopped. She fingered the line of her silk dress and cast one last cursory glance around the room before raising her foot onto one of the lower bookshelves. Her heel clicked against the faux volumes below as she quickly pulled up the layers of her dress and petticoats. Silk ran against silk until all that was left was a pale white leg showing in the warm candlelight through the sheerness of her shift.

She would have to be quick. John would already be calling her a carriage after seeing her leave the room with Mr. Russell. Angelica's dressmaker, Madame Depardieu, had not only lowered the neckline of this gown, but she had also added a secret pocket. Stitched into the underside of her petticoat, it was the perfect place to hide her newly-acquired blunt. Unlike her pockets which could be reached normally, this compartment was only accessible from the underside of the gown.

Now came the tricky part—the buttons. Thankfully, the Lord had blessed Angelica with a particularly long set of fingers and, despite the tiniest of buttons and the difficult positioning on the inside of her petticoat, she soon had the compartment undone. She folded the notes and laid them flat in the pocket so that they would lie unseen against her body for the journey home.

She was just fastening the last button when she heard the door open. Her raven-haired head shot up, and her large eyes darted in the direction of the intruder. No one had ever entered when she had been in here alone before. What was Mr. Russell thinking? He always left her in peace until she left of her own accord.

So shocked was she, she failed to remove her foot from its perch on the bookshelf and cover herself before a gentleman entered—a gentleman that was *not* Mr. Russell. At least, that is if you could call the man who entered a gentleman at all. The man in question practically fell into the room, sloshing the tankard of ale in his hand and taking more than a few seconds to find his footing.

Angelica watched with horrified fascination as the tousled hair escaping the pathetic ribbon at the back of his neck flicked up and down while he gained his balance. For a moment she wondered if he would merely stumble back out again, quite unaware of her presence. But fortune would not smile upon Angelica a second time tonight.

In spite of his graceless entrance and obvious inebriation, the man's eyes were exceedingly quick. As he righted himself, they made contact with a heeled shoe, a pleasingly long leg beneath the flimsiest of materials, and a gathering of skirts. His eyes continued their journey upwards, over her bodice, her neck, and then they stilled at those indefinable blue eyes.

In the odd pause that followed, a cat-like smile slowly unfurled across the young man's face. Angelica threw down her skirts and stepped back.

"I say..." was all the gentleman offered. He half-raised the tankard as if in salute, and Angelica could only be thankful that he had knocked the door shut during his imbalance. Or was she thankful? She took another step back, hitting the panelling of the wall.

She did not recognise the man, but he was undeniably handsome. Aware that she was looking him over, his boyish face gained a mischievousness. His green eyes twinkled merrily at her, lingering—to her utter infuriation—on her lips. He stumbled towards a book-lined wall and rested an unsteady elbow upon one of the shelves, leaning jauntily on one leg and most clearly making himself at home.

"I say..." he repeated himself, but he did not move towards her as Angelica had feared.

Her wits finally returning, she put some ice into her stare. "You say what, sir?"

She was buying time. She was not yet sure how to work the situation to her advantage. Should she play upon his intoxication and hope a little flirtation would gain her access to the door? Or should she give him a set-down and storm out, risking that he might attempt to stop her? If it had been someone she knew, she might have been able to guess which would be the best course of action.

As it was, she could not rely on John's appearance—he always waited downstairs for her with the carriage.

"I say," the man responded affably, as if they were acquaintances encountering each other during a promenade through

Town, "that is a rather clever trick you have there." He gestured to the compartment recently concealed in her skirts.

"I don't know what you mean," she replied too quickly, her heart still fluttering.

The gentleman merely smiled and shrugged his shoulders. As though he had not just learnt a valuable secret. As though he did not intend to rob her. As though...well, as though he cared not a whit for the precarious position in which he had found her. Apparently he was not going to take advantage of it —but neither was he planning to ignore it.

Angelica was momentarily stumped. But then, choosing the course of action that had worked most successfully in the past, she took two small steps forward. She raised her head so that her neck was shown to the best advantage, relaxed her full lips so that they pouted attractively, and brought a hand up to play with the cravat encircling the man's neck. Teasing at the folds, she noted that although she had first guessed his age to be just above twenty, a closer inspection showed him to be nearer thirty.

"And just whom do I have the pleasure of addressing?" Her tone dripped with honey, though her eyes still searched his face shrewdly for any sign as to his intentions.

"Pleasure?"

For a moment he looked dashing. She found herself looking no longer at his eyes but at his lips as they curved in a pleasing smile. Her stomach fluttered.

"Is that what you feel?" He was leaning closer now, sending the smell of cloves and ale wafting toward her.

The spellbound moment ended rather abruptly. The gentleman's elbow, which up until now had been wedged between two rows of false books, slipped. The jolt of movement turned his enticing lean into a headlong plunge towards Angelica's bosom.

Angelica immediately assumed he was attempting to steal her winnings—or worse.

"Oh...oh, I am sorry!" he managed, pulling himself out of her décolletage and into balance.

But even his boyish green eyes could not save him.

Angelica delivered a resounding slap across his face. Gathering up her skirts, she marched from the room without a backwards glance. If she had looked behind her, she would have seen a gentleman utterly bemused, his mouth hanging open like a catfish while he stared after the angel who had departed so suddenly.

Keep reading *Fool Me Twice* by picking up your copy now:

philippajanekeyworth.com/FMT

philippajanekeyworth.com/FMT

philippajanekeyworth.com/ADD

philippajanekeyworth.com/LOW

philippajanekeyworth.com/DOD

REGENCY ROMANCES

philippajanekeyworth.com/TWR

philippajanekeyworth.com/TUE